CHRISTMAS AT THE LITTLE VILLAGE SCHOOL

Working at a tiny village school in rural Yorkshire has its own unique set of challenges — but when Lydia Knight and Jake Immingham are tasked with getting the children to put on a Christmas play for the local elderly people's home, they know they're in for a tricky term! From choreographing sugar plum dance routines to dealing with reindeer costume malfunctions, Lydia realises that, even as a teacher, she isn't past being taught a couple of things — and one of those things is a much-needed lesson in Christmas spirit.

(

SPECIAL MESSAGE TO READERS

THE ULVERSCROFT FOUNDATION
(registered UK charity number 264873)

was established in 1972 to provide funds for research, diagnosis and treatment of eye diseases. Examples of major projects funded by the Ulverscroft Foundation are:-

- The Children's Eye Unit at Moorfields Eye Hospital, London
- The Ulverscroft Children's Eye Unit at Great Ormond Street Hospital for Sick Children
- Funding research into eye diseases and treatment at the Department of Ophthalmology, University of Leicester
- The Ulverscroft Vision Research Group, Institute of Child Health
- Twin operating theatres at the Western Ophthalmic Hospital, London
- The Chair of Ophthalmology at the Royal Australian College of Ophthalmologists

You can help further the work of the Foundation by making a donation or leaving a legacy. Every contribution is gratefully received. If you would like to help support the Foundation or require further information, please contact:

THE ULVERSCROFT FOUNDATION
The Green, Bradgate Road, Anstey
Leicester LE7 7FU, England
Tel: (0116) 236 4325

website: www.foundation.ulverscroft.com

JANE LOVERING

CHRISTMAS AT THE LITTLE VILLAGE SCHOOL

Complete and Unabridged

LINFORD
Leicester

First published in Great Britain in 2017 by
Choc Lit Limited
Surrey

First Linford Edition
published 2018
Choc Lit Limited
Surrey

A catalogue record for this book is available
from the British Library.

ISBN 978–1–4448–3905–0

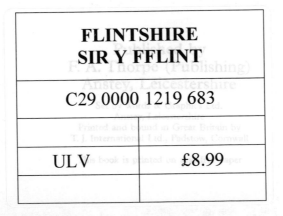

Dedicated to the memory of my mum, Betty, who always made Christmas such a great event. RIP.

Acknowledgements

I'd just like to use this space to acknowledge all the teachers out there. I only teach adults, and goodness knows, they can be a handful at times, so I can only imagine how tough things can get faced by a classroom full. And, at this time of year, I particularly admire all those hard-working primary teachers, trying to teach, prepare for Christmas, and deal with their own families!

Thank you also to the Tasting Panel readers who passed this book: Vanessa W, Janine N, Michelle M, Ruth N, Melissa C, Kathryn M, Yvonne G, Els E, Melissa C, Melissa B, Jo O, Hilary B and Cordy S.

1

October 26th

There are a few things that a head teacher can say to you to make your heart stop. 'OFSTED are coming' is one. Another is the one that Alan let slip, putting his head around the door to my classroom while I was tidying up. 'Lydia, have you thought about doing a Christmas play this year? Only White Rose want to get together an outing for their residents, and they were asking . . . ' And then, like the Cheshire Cat, he was gone, only instead of a smile he left a lingering smell of Old Spice overlaying the usual 'small children with varying approaches to toilet hygiene, glue and crayons' scent of the room and the whiff of silage which wafted in from the farm down the lane.

I had to give my whiteboard a slow

and therapeutic clean to let my heart-rate slow down. *Christmas play? Is he mad? Well, he's the Head of a rural primary school with only three teachers, one of whom is so new he's still got the plastic on, so, yes, probably.* I wrote tomorrow's date very carefully in the top left-hand corner of the board, so that nobody could say I wasn't prepared and had underlined it twice in two colours, when another head appeared. This wasn't a Head of School, just a body-part with a half-untied plait swinging over one shoulder above a bright fuchsia cardigan, the pockets of which were stuffed with tissues, Freddo frog chocolate bars, pencils and wet wipes. Irina was a one-woman emergency kit, taught Reception, Year One and Two, and was my best friend — despite the fact that she bullied me mercilessly. 'Lydia, it is time to go home now. Go.' The rest of her came around the door and she flapped her hands at me.

'Alan wants us to do a Christmas play.' I didn't see why the misery shouldn't be spread as widely and as fast as possible. 'So the residents of White Rose, you know, the old people's home, can come and see it. Has he mentioned it to you? Or to . . . ?' I waved a hand in the direction of the other classroom, where Years Five and Six worked under the tutelage of Jake 'Mister' Immingham; a man I hadn't even had a proper conversation with yet, despite the fact that he'd started at the school in September. I had, however, brought up the subjects of door handle heights, pencil distribution and Year Six's persistent occupation of the play house at the end of the school field. But nothing personal. Oh no.

'No?' Irina sat on one of the tables. 'What is this all about? What is wrong with the usual Christmas party? I *like* the Christmas party. We have never done a Christmas play.'

'Didn't think so.' I'd been at the school for five years to Irina's seven. Term ended in December in a riot of Jammy Dodgers and crisps, and everyone went home at two. Well, everyone except me; usually, I stayed behind to scrub the jam out of the reading corner carpet and to get everything straight for the beginning of next term. With the cutbacks in education that were so rife, our current cleaner only just had time to run a mop over the lino and do something arcane with industrial detergent in the toilets. 'I don't think he quite realises what's involved.'

'He's got to you too?' The voice came from the corridor. Jake Immingham was still, as Rory Scott (Year Four and a wannabe rap artist, despite the fact that his parents ran a tea shop in the village and he was destined to be up to his elbows in scones from the minute he turned sixteen) would have it, 'in da house'.

'He told Lydia. I can still plead ignorance,' Irina said into the gap between the door and the hallway. 'What are we going to do?'

'At a guess, we're going to do a Christmas play.' The door opened wider and Jake came in to my classroom. He looked around at the model village that we'd made last half-term and I felt the skin at the back of my neck prickle. Although there was nothing derisory in his look, I was working on what I'd say if he even *suggested* there was anything wrong with the fourteen cardboard box houses of varying size (one per student), laid out along a carefully drawn roadway. 'It might be fun.' He sat down on the table next to Irina and I heard the plastic groan.

Jake Immingham was not built for primary school teaching. He was built for something that took place on a muddy field between men in shorts, involving lots of shouting and throwing. Football or rugby or hurling or one of the uniquely Yorkshire sports that we tried out every now and again with the children, and usually resolved never to do again, once we'd mopped up the blood. He was all shoulders and legs, with messy dark hair, stubble that never seemed to turn into a beard, and an attitude. Years Five and Six adored him.

I wanted to send him bog walking on the high moors and see if he came back quite so smug. Even the way he entered a room made me feel defensive. He might be easy on the eye, but that didn't mean he had any right to be quite so smiley and jocular and all round *nice*! Why couldn't he have the decency to be a tetchy bugger and make my life easier?

Irina sighed and looked at her watch, dramatically. I knew she was doing it dramatically because there was a, quite frankly, bloody enormous clock on the wall by the whiteboard. 'I must go home,' she said. 'I have a family to feed. Jake, Lydia, you may decide on the play and I will go along with what you think.' She stood up and her pockets swung like gun holsters at her sides. 'But nothing too complicated, please. Reception are really only suited to snowflakes and 'Away in a Manger', and we are still having a few toilet issues, so not a long performance, if you can.'

'I don't think we're quite ready for the 'Ring of the Nibelungs' yet,' Jake said dryly. I wasn't sure if he was being sarcastic, or if he didn't expect either of us to know our Wagner.

'I'm sure Year Six would be up for Gotterdammerung,' I said, pointedly.

'As long as it comes in a format for PlayStation.' He gave me a sudden grin, at which I narrowed my eyes. Did he think I needed winning over? Well, good. Let him carry on thinking that.

Irina raised an eyebrow. 'Yes. Very good. But I am still going home. You two, who have no lives to speak of, may agree this between you, but there is a chicken stew in the slow cooker and Pawel will have picked up the children by now, so I don't care. See you tomorrow.' And then she gave me a look that was a cross between a grin and a glare. 'And remember: not too long, with snowflakes in.' She sauntered out of my classroom, hitching a cardigan pocket on the door handle as she passed through and having to return to unhook it, swearing in Polish as she did so. It was entirely her own fault, those door handles had trained me out of hip-level pockets and loose sleeves by term one, day three.

The room suddenly felt very empty. Outside I could hear birdsong and the cows waiting to go through the milking parlour calling from the yard, and I reminded myself again how lucky I was to be in such a lovely rural environment when I could have been in an inner city school with thirty-five children to a class. Instead, Irina had twelve, I had fourteen and Jake had eleven. We had thirty-four children in the entire school. It should have been idyllic. It *was* idyllic.

'Are you in a hurry to get back?' Jake stood up. The tables were low enough that adults got cramp of the thigh sitting on them for too long. 'Only, we could talk about the play now, if you like.' He went to the window and looked out. It was just after five and the October sun was sinking fast towards

8

twilight, slithering down behind the hills that bulked out the landscape, and smearing the sky with an improbable yellowish orange like the display of paintings Irina had pegged on her wall. Year One knew a thing or two about painting a Yorkshire Moors sunset, basically use all the colours on the 'bright' side of the paint-box, and a big brush.

'Mrs Wilkinson will be wanting to lock up,' I said. 'She must have finished the toilets by now. Or dissolved in the backwash of Jeyes Fluid.' I picked up my bag and my papers. I'd got seven Year Three poems to read through tonight and mark, and a lesson on the classification of living things to sort out. Plus, Jake Immingham and his careful chinos and chequered shirt made my skin twitch. I needed the slow walk home with the darkness beginning to pucker around me and the cool touch of the start of an early frost swiping the tips of my ears.

'Why don't you like me?' He was still

staring out of the window. 'I mean, if it's not rude of me to ask.'

'I don't dislike you.' My voice sounded stiff and slightly distant. 'I don't know you.'

'No.' Then he turned around from the window. 'Why don't you come over to the farm? We can talk about the play, get the details thrashed out before Alan three-line-whips us into *A Christmas Carol* and the Cratchits have to have nine children so that all Year One and Two get a go on stage.'

I stared at him. 'Why do we have to do that in a farmyard?'

'Because that's where I'm staying until I buy a house up here. Not in the yard, in the farm. Bed and breakfast. And, quite often, a hearty dinner and three snacks a day, because Mrs Dobson is rather old-fashioned and believes that a single man is incapable of surviving unless there is someone to do his washing and provide him with potato-based meals.' He looked down at his sturdy frame. 'I was nine stone when I came to Roseberry Farm.'

'I can't.'

'Oh, okay. Well how about an early start tomorrow then? School is open from seven, you're usually here round about then, I'm only two minutes away over the field . . . ?'

'I have marking to do.'

He gave me a very direct look. It was a look that had trained up on eleven-year-old boys starting to get the hang of testosterone. 'Now or in the morning?'

'Both.' I tried to return the look but my eyes wouldn't focus on his face. They kept sliding sideways and staring at the picture of Wordsworth and his daffodils that was pinned on the wall to the left. 'I'm sorry but I have to go now.'

I slung my big, leather document case over my shoulder by its long strap and clutched my bag to my chest, hoping he'd get the message. Actually, hoping he had piles of lesson prep to do too and was putting it off by talking to me, and that any moment now he'd remember that he was behind with his fractions marking.

He did an odd sideways nod, like half-acceptance and half-annoyance. 'We need to talk about it sometime. There's not that many weeks left before we break up for Christmas and we'll need rehearsals, costume fittings, learning songs, all that. After all, it will probably be the highlight of the older people's Christmas, seeing the cute children performing, you wouldn't want to let them down, would you?'

That was so far below the belt that it was practically knee level. 'Well, if we can do something with not too many words in, that will help.' I still had my bag tight against my chest. It was actually squashing my boobs and I had to relax a little bit or risk spraining a nipple. 'The mums will all do costumes, given enough notice, if we can keep those simple . . . Are you trying to lure me into talking about the play?'

'No. Maybe. Little bit.'

The smile in his voice made me look at his face again. He had laugh lines that creased the skin around his brown eyes like tissue paper and made me realise that he was older than he looked. Not the mid-twenties wannabe, sprinting up through the ranks to the coveted Head of School role, although, given Alan's perpetually worried expression and egg-stained tie, I wasn't sure quite *why* it was so coveted. 'Well I'm sorry, I have to go. We can arrange a meeting to talk it over, if you like.' My heart was beating so hard in my ears that it sounded as though I had a tiny animal trapped in my bag, trying to kick its way free.

I swung around towards the door and he jumped up to open it for me. This left me with no choice but to go through and out into the corridor. I'd been hoping that he'd take the hint and go, leave me in my quiet classroom to gather my thoughts, but no chance. He compounded his error by walking with me to the main front door. 'If you come up with any ideas . . . I mean, for the play? I'm always in by seven-thirty, we could put our heads together, come up with something to keep Alan happy.'

I swiped my key card. 'I've got marking to do.' I pushed open the front door and felt the chill of autumn needling in under the residual warmth of the day. He hesitated for a moment and the thought that he might offer to walk me home crossed my mind, so I stormed off out into the shadowy evening without giving him chance to say or do anything else.

2

Out of the school, turn right, and then there was nothing but country lanes. Hawthorn hedges threaded with berries and filmy cobwebs lined the quiet stretch of tarmac that led from nowhere very much and stretched up like an arthritic arm onto the moors that overhung us in a bucolic cuddle. Heavington wasn't even much of a settlement these days; the big old house that had presided over the estate was now the White Rose Sheltered Accommodation and Residential Care Home for the Elderly and the estate houses were mostly weekend and holiday cottages. There was a small post office (Sara Cowton, Year Two and her little brother James, Reception), and the redoubtable Rory Scott's family tea shop. A few of the smaller cottages were still family homes for workers on local farms, who had yet to settle for long enough to produce children, and the old Dower House was occupied by the Grace family and their six children (Timothy and Oscar, Year Six, Aurora, Year Four, Atticus, Year One, Celeste, Reception, and the baby, who they all called Bo-Bo; we had no idea of its gender or real name). The rest of the children at school were driven in by parents from outlying villages or the suburbs of the local town, where the oversubscribed primary was sprawling its way into Portacabins and the lunch hall, and was therefore seen as less desirable than our bijou little schoolette, despite its positive OFSTED ranking, state-of-the-art computer room and field trips.

I breathed deeply. There was a heavy smell of mud in the air, unsurprisingly, as tractors had been up and down the road all day bearing their shiny anchors of plough, glazed with wet earth. There had been a procession of boys at lunchtime all willing and eager to tell anyone who would listen about the makes and models of tractors and stories of various dads and uncles and their ability with a sixteen-furrow reversible; it was one of the ways we knew that autumn was well underway. That and the hundred and forty pounds of blackberries that the children brought in for us teachers, having been out picking with their families at the weekends. I now knew every conceivable recipe that could contain blackberries and was thinking of starting some blackberry gin. In fact, the mere thought of having to put on a Christmas play made the gin sound very appealing.

Further along the road, where the lane turned into a single track, lay my house. A converted village hall, built in the austerity times of the Great War out of corrugated iron and left-overs from farm buildings. It sat at the junction of the road and a bridleway, which snaked off over the fields and down towards the distant woods that had also once belonged to the Big House, and jangled its roof in high winds. I went inside and shut the door with a metallic twang against what remained of the day. Irina always said that the noise was like a bell tolling the death knell to my social life, but that's Irina for you. She thought that, as a single woman, I should be out every night not 'shut away in a metal box partying like it's 1549'. I put it down to jealousy, since she had small children and all her parties involved jelly.

With a wanton disregard for my electricity bill, because I had to be allowed to splurge somewhere, I'd left a small lamp on when I went to work, so indoors was softly lit with a relaxing pink light. The inside of the hall had been panelled in old wood, which I'd left when I'd converted the building (well, I say 'I', really I'd supervised a bunch of men in fluorescent jackets, all apparently called Dave) and the polished panels reflected the light gently as I peeled off my coat and went into the kitchen to put the kettle on. The vaguest smell of cow still lingered, because I strongly suspected that the panelling had been taken from planks previously used in a barn, and every time the word 'recycling' came up at school I got a synaesthesic whiff of muck, but I loved them. I polished them all every weekend, and, through Saturday Mr Sheen won out, but by Sunday evening the warm, organic smell was back and I'd learned to live with it.

While I waited for the kettle to boil I went through into my bedroom, which had been the old hall kitchen and the mirror I used to do my make-up covered a large plastered square where the village tea urn had once stood. In there I stripped off my teacher persona; the carefully cut trousers, the stain-resistant blouse and all the accoutrements of my day-to-day life. I put on my saggy yoga bottoms, a T shirt and then, because the heating was taking a while to warm the autumn out of the air, my dressing-gown, and cautiously made my way back into the main house again.

Apart from the bedroom and bathroom, my house was pretty much all one room. The breakfast bar divided the living space from the kitchen and meant I could lean on it and see out of the front window into the darkening road beyond as I made my cup of tea. Letting my eyes unfocus, I rested both elbows on the worktop, sipped and stared through the narrow panes of wartime glass, which made the outlines of the trees on the other side of the road wobble like an enthusiastic nine-year-old on a narrow plank. I loved this place. And, on a rural primary teacher's salary, it was a miracle I could afford anything, so I spun it to everyone I talked to into a detached residence with far-reaching views rather than a basic, small tin box with windows and a roof that made heavy rain sound like gunfire. You really didn't want to be in there during a hailstorm without ear defenders, but never mind. It was mine. The place I relaxed. The *only* place I relaxed. The only place I allowed myself those little day-dreamy fantasies, the ones I didn't even tell Irina about, where Jake Immingham noticed me as more than a fellow teacher. The fantasies in which I could let him notice me, didn't have to maintain this façade of not caring what he thought of me, or keep him at arm's length.

And then I had to give myself a good sturdy talking to. *You're a good teacher. You have a life. You don't need a man like Jake Immingham. You don't need a man, full stop. Hell, you don't need anybody. That's what cats are for.*

Between the rising steam from the mug and the dimness of the lamp I couldn't be sure, but I almost thought I could see a shape outside, something hovering uncertainly in the road outside the house. I moved my head up and down to cancel out the uneven glass, yes, there was definitely something there, darker than the rising night, a shadow against the background of

21

hedge and stile and hunting gate.

The tension was back now, between my shoulder blades. That tension that only really left me when I was alone, surrounded by my own things in my own space. The tension that I carried like a rucksack full of bricks, so ever present that I usually forgot it was there until something like this made me aware of it, and that made me angry. Okay, so this was probably a stray cow from the farm or a horse and rider that had taken the bridleway and got lost in a night that had descended more rapidly than expected, but even so, wasn't I allowed *any* peace?

'Who's there?' I flung open the door, letting the light of the lamps spill out to illuminate the muddy bit of trackway immediately outside. As the light flowed out, the smell of mud came in, and then it was followed by a voice.

'I just had a brilliant idea and I thought . . . '

Jake Immingham. Still in his 'teaching' clothes. The thought that he might have followed me back, been behind me as I walked home, made my neck break out into a sweat. 'I said we could talk about it at school.' I gripped my front door, the metal chilly against my fingers but a welcome antidote to the heat that was sweeping up from my knees and was probably colouring my face. 'You didn't need to come to my house.'

'Wow, this is your house? I thought it . . . ' and then adulthood cut back in. 'Sorry. Yes, no, I mean. I didn't have to come but I just wanted to run it by you before I forgot all about it. Sorry.' He half-turned, then paused. 'Are you sure this is your house? You aren't hiding out here or something?'

'Are you reading Anthony Horowitz to your class again? Why would I be hiding out? What from?'

'You have to admit it's a bit . . . ' Jake stared over his shoulder at my house. 'Hutty,' he finished, after obviously having groped for the right word. 'Hut-like,' he modified.

'Only on the outside,' and my tone

was so chilly that I could swear it drew down a hoar frost to crisp the leaves around us.

'Well I can only see the outside.' Jake's reasonableness made him sound as though he was talking to a ten-year-old. 'To be fair.'

I took a deep breath again. The tension in my back and shoulders felt strange, not like the usual rucksack of horror that I carried, this was warmer. As though a small animal had crawled in and was heating my spine. Good grief, was I actually *enjoying* having him at a disadvantage like this? 'I'm not inviting you in. It's late and I've got work to do. As I think I told you. Repeatedly.'

'You're wearing your dressing-gown.'

'I'm marking classwork. I'm a teacher not a TV presenter, what does it matter what I'm wearing?' I *knew* I was being unnecessarily sharp, I mean, it didn't really matter one way or the other what he thought I was doing. I could have been unravelling cats or hand-carving my family motto into the floor. Hell, *I* didn't care, so why should he? And he'd come to talk about work. But snippy was what I did. It was how . . . it was *who* I was. Plus I hated being caught out of my teaching wear, having him point it out made it even worse. 'And I have to go and do it now. We can talk at school tomorrow.'

I leaned my weight into the door and it began to close, slowly with a rusty squeak that called out for a butler with a lisp and, possibly, scuttling rats. It was a good noise, a noise that said absolutely definitely *go away, this conversation is over.* And, sometimes, *I don't need double glazing.* It never failed to get rid of unwanted callers. Except today, when the combination of my weight and the angle I was pushing from meant that the door accelerated in its closure and I fell against it, so it closed with a slam that was more emphatic than I had intended, and I hit my head on it as I went down. The noise was catastrophic, and the metallic ringing went on for so long that I wasn't sure whether it was acoustic or concussion, as I lay on the floor.

Eventually the noise of the door died away, to be replaced by the sound of the letterbox flap being lifted and then a voice. 'Are you okay? Did something happen?'

'No.'

The flap rattled again. 'You're on the floor.'

'Today is really your day for stating the obvious, isn't it?' I hoisted myself to my elbows. 'It's nothing. I'm fine.'

'On the floor, in your dressing-gown.'

'And fine.' The words came out clipped short by my gritted teeth. Actually I wasn't sure I was fine, I could feel the sting of a cut and the warm drip of blood on the side of my face. 'So go away.'

A moment of quiet. The chilly evening breeze puffing through the slit in the door told me that he hadn't let the letterbox close yet and was presumably still peering through the slot. I tried to hunch myself against the bottom of the door so he couldn't see me, but there wasn't quite room. The fluff of my dressing-gown snagged on the matting like Velcro.

'I was thinking about that poem. The one about Father Christmas coming down the chimney while everyone is asleep?' Jake was talking perfectly normally, as though we were having a face-to-face conversation. 'Superficially creepy, and any other time a big bloke breaking into your house at night would be an arrestable offence, but I guess we can let that go, as it's Christmas. The kids could act it out and we could have a narrator.'

'Do you mean *The Night Before Christmas?*' Actually, that wasn't a bad idea. Fairly short, not too many parts, and Alexandra Houghton, whose mother drove a Range Rover and, I suspected, gave her private tuition, had been playing the part of narrator since she was in Year Three. 'Reception could be sugar plums, I suppose. Or mice. Sugar plums would probably be better, less sewing, because tails are always a problem. They stand on the ends and pull them off.'

There was another moment of quiet, which gave me the opportunity to properly appreciate the ridiculousness of our situation, discussing the Christmas play through a slot in my front door, whilst I lay on the floor with blood slowly seeping down my cheek, trying to pretend this was normal.

'I don't know it *that* well,' Jake finally admitted. 'Just the bit about 'Happy Christmas to all and to all a good night'. Is that in it? Or am I thinking about something else? Anyway. Something to think about.'

'Yes.'

'Are you *sure* you're all right?'

As I was lying right up against the door, and my dressing-gown was acting as a very effective draught excluder, if I *hadn't* been all right there was no physical way he would get into the house without shoving me back against the wall. 'Positive.' And then, through gritted teeth again, 'thank you.'

'You're allowed *not* to be all right, you know.' His voice was softer now. 'It's not an admission of anything.'

Oh, that's where you are wrong, Mister Immingham. 'I'll be fine. I'll have a look at *The Night Before Christmas*, maybe draw up a cast list, see if it's practicable.' I pushed my elbows underneath me to prop myself clear of the floor.

'After you've done your marking, obviously.' He sounded a bit curt now. Was he embarrassed about his persistence that I might need help?

'Oh. Yes. After that, of course.'

The letterbox flap dropped and I heard him sigh, even through the door. 'Goodnight, Lydia,' he said, and it was said half-quietly, as though I wasn't really meant to hear.

'Goodnight, Mister Immingham,' I replied, equally quietly. Whether he heard or not I wasn't sure, but his footsteps were definitely audible as he headed back down the rough track, the squelch and suck of the covering layer of mud against his trendy trainers. I slid myself over to the sofa and used it to pull myself upright. I put a hand to my face and was slightly shocked when I realised that it wasn't blood trickling down my cheek now. It was tears.

3

'Miss, Miss!' Thomas Hipgood's hand was so high in the air that his bottom had left his seat. 'Miss!'

'Yes, Thomas?' Jackie, my redoubtable teaching assistant, who had been working with Nathan Jemison (needed some help in class, was under assessment for ASD, but a complete wizard on the football field), went over. I carried on writing on the whiteboard. CONSTELLATIONS. Their homework was to look at the night sky and try to identify the Great Bear.

'Not you, Miss, *other* Miss! Miss!' Thomas was on his feet now, his hand wobbling with eagerness.

'What is it?' I turned back around.

'Why is it a bear, Miss? My dad says it's called the Plough, but it doesn't look like a plough either, does it?'

'It's supposed to look like an old-fashioned plough, Thomas. Let's see.' I flicked through the computer until I found a picture of an ox pulling a wooden plough and put it up on the screen. 'Like that'.

There was a general snort of disbelief. These were mostly farming children, and even those from the town had seen enough heavy-duty equipment rumbling past the school gate to know that this thing bore as much resemblance to a plough as I did to Zoella.

'Why's it got a cow on it?' Rory asked. 'Cows can't pull ploughs, that's stupid. They'd fall over.'

'My grandad's got horses that pull a plough sometimes,' Rebecca Francis put in.

'Well, horses aren't like cows, are they? Horses pull carts. Cows don't. 'Cos that would be mental.'

I opened my mouth to start a small sub-lesson on the history of farming, which might not come under the heading of The Universe but was clearly going to come as an eye-opener to the iPhone generation, when there was a brief tap at the door and Jake appeared.

'Hello you lot,' he said.

The hero-worship radiated off my class and filled the room much like the smell of chips from the dining hall was doing. 'Hello Mister Immingham!' they chanted. Even Nathan looked up and smiled.

'I just need to borrow Miss Knight for a moment, if that's all right?' He spoke as if asking the class's permission, but he was really asking Jackie, who blushed slightly at the eye contact. I didn't know why.

I raised an eyebrow at him and looked at my whiteboard, but he ignored me, so I looked hopefully at Jackie. She misread my hope completely. 'Of course. We'll get on with drawing our Night Skies, won't we?' Her tone could only be described as pert. Clearly another one under the spell of Jake Immingham and his floppy hair. I scowled at her but she gave me a bright smile and came to the front of the class. 'He's lush,' she whispered to me as I handed her the remote control for the computer projector. 'You should so give him a go.'

'Don't you start,' I whispered back.

'Wouldn't dare.' But she waggled her eyebrows at me as I picked up my bag and followed Jake out of the classroom. We passed his room, which surprised me. I'd thought he needed my help with one of his class, but they were all head-down, enthusiastically and quietly working through something in their books and, I had to admit it but only to myself, I was impressed. Year Six, particularly, were a lively bunch, so to see them all so engaged was surprising. I wondered if he'd sedated them somehow.

'They're drawing designs for the Christmas decorations they're going to make,' he said, filling the quiet that lay between us as we walked down the corridor. 'Alan is keeping an eye on them. Anyway. I thought kidnapping you was the best way to get you to slow down long enough for us to talk about this play business.' He stopped at the door to Alan's office. 'It's only going to be for a couple of minutes, you don't need to panic.'

'I wasn't panicking.' To prove it I stepped into the office.

'Just to be clear, I was using the term 'kidnap' in its figurative sense.' Jake followed me in. 'Everyone knows you're here and everything, which would be a rubbish kidnap attempt, if you think about it.'

'Are you trying to 'put me at my ease' or something?' I leaned against Alan's desk. As ever it was strewn with papers and his computer smelled of burning electrical components. There was a headed letter under my hand and I couldn't help notice it came from the White Rose home. 'Because you don't need to bother.'

'Really?' He slouched half in the doorway. 'Whenever you see me you get this kind of 'hunted' thing going on, as if you think I'm peering through your bedroom window at night. Which I'm not, obviously,' he added quickly. 'I mean, you can check with Mrs Dobson. In every night by six for dinner, otherwise she'd refuse to feed me. Actually she probably wouldn't, and I'd find her sliding sandwiches under my bedroom door, but that's beside the point. I just want you to feel less . . . whatever it is you feel. How's the face?'

I didn't want to, but my hand rose up to touch my cheek as though I was a marionette and he was pulling my string. 'Fine.' It was still slightly sore but the bruising had gone down in the last couple of days. 'The play?' The letter under my hand contained words like 'so looking forward' and 'some residents with no family'. It couldn't have invoked more guilt without actually having been slightly burned at the edges, and with a few tear-stains on the page. Its mere presence was like having an injured puppy in the room.

Jake made a movement, as though he had been about to lay a finger on my injured cheek, but then went back to his leaning against the doorframe. 'All right, I get the message. I'm going to stop being nice to you now, just fair warning. I've only got so much niceness in me and it's severely eroded by ten- and eleven-year-olds on a daily basis, so it will be a relief, actually, not to have to try to be pleasant to someone who clearly wants me packed up in a shoe box and sent home.'

His tone was perfectly pleasant, but the words stung. 'I don't need you to be nice to me. Civil will do. Now, about the play.'

'Actually Lydia, even civility is straining a bit under the weight of your obvious dislike, but hey ho, professional to the last, I've been reading *The Night Before Christmas* and I've done a bit of a cast list, thought you should give it a look over before I suggest it to the kids. Nothing radical, but I thought we ought to get things moving.' He was looking away now, staring out at Alan's unprepossessing view of the PE equipment shed. There was a set to his shoulders, an almost defensive angle under the approved 'teacher' shirt. I'd often wondered if male teachers all bought their clothes at the same shop; there was a similarity to them that bordered on the uniform. He actually sounded more hurt than anything, when I considered his words. I wondered why, I hadn't really been anything other than factual.

He'd typed the cast list. I was impressed, it showed a level of preparation that I was unused to outside my own work. 'Rory for the lead man, yes, I think he could do that. Sugar plums, oh, I see you've got reindeer, that's nice.' I was half speaking to myself as I ran my eye down the list, then, 'oh.'

'Yes, I thought it might be nice for Alexandra to have an actual part. She told me she was bored with always being the narrator and she wanted to do something where she could dance. She has, apparently and not altogether surprisingly, got her own tap shoes.'

'But you've put me as narrator.'

Jake looked at me. 'Yes. Problem?'

'I don't go on stage. I do the backstage stuff. Mopping up the sugar plums. Straightening the reindeer antlers, that sort of thing.' I knew he was watching me but I kept my eyes on the piece of paper. 'Getting Father Christmas out on cue.'

'Irina can do that though, can't she? If we have Reception as sugar plums, then Year One and Two can be the children all snug in their beds — I thought a bit of theatrical stretching and yawning first — so there won't be a lot of wrangling.'

'What about you?'

'I'm props, costume and technical. Lights and sound and so forth. You'll be fine, Lydia. You've got a lovely speaking voice, very Radio Four, and we need someone who can enunciate over the sound of 'there's my mummy', phones going off because they weren't switched to silent, and twenty screaming toddlers. Sorry if I sound a bit jaded there but did my PGCE in a primary with six hundred pupils and the nativity from hell.' He gave me a sideways smile. 'I sort of envisaged you just off centre stage, reading from a big book?'

I put the paper down, firmly. It covered the letter from the White Rose home. 'I don't go on stage. If I really have to be the narrator, and I would only do it under protest, I can narrate from the wings.'

'No, you'd be all muffled.'

'I can enunciate. As you said. Now, if that's everything covered, I need to get back to my class.'

'But I . . . '

'Or maybe we would be better getting Alexandra to do it?'

'I've sort of promised her that she could be the moon. I thought a quick tippetty tap across the stage would be okay and not too irritating. I think she's got ideas of a full-on routine, jazz hands

40

and everything, but we haven't got time for that, plus the reindeer will be getting impatient.'

I got to the doorway, where he was still propped against the frame. 'So you've already discussed this with your class? Without asking me first?' I straightened my back to bring me nearer to his height. 'That wasn't very fair, was it?' He smelled nice, my nose told me. A smell I wasn't used to; not the normal pencil sharpenings and Plasticine smell that we carried with us at all times, marking us out as primary teachers as surely as if we'd worn badges. His smell was sharp and clean and made me think of fresh air and running through fields on a windy day. The thought jabbed me in the ribs and startled my breath. 'I have to get back.'

'Of course.' He moved to one side to let me get past, and the scent bubbled up behind his words. I'd never be able to hear anyone say 'of course' again without the memory of that outdoorsy sort of smell coming back to haunt me.

'Just thought I'd give you a quick heads-up, Lydia. We'll start work on it next week, maybe during English? A proper read-through and casting and everything? And I want you to notice that I'm still being civil and polite here, although every line of your body seems to say that you want to hit me?'

I had to smile at that. 'I wouldn't hit you.'

'Pelt me with whiteboard markers then.' He gave what might have been a small grin.

'I don't not like you,' I said it quietly. 'I just think we should be professional. Because we work together, it doesn't mean we have to be plaiting one another's hair and comparing Fingerlings.'

The grin got just the tiniest bit wider. 'You really do need to mix more with people over the age of nine. And anyway, that's not really true is it? You're friends with Irina. And you're wonderful to the kids, and they're your *job*. In fact, you *love* the kids, I've seen you with them, remember.'

'Children are different.'

There was a moment of silence. Well, as near to silence as one can ever get in a school; there were the usual, distant raised voices, the whine of the photocopier, the outside hum of a hedgetrimmer. In the office, just Jake and me, it was quiet. I picked up the cast list again, and between my fingers, the pages crackled.

It was a situation that begged one of us to speak, but neither of us did, and I squeezed past him, him and his outdoor smell and his sportsman frame, and went back to my class.

4

At lunch, I was on playground duty. Jackie and our solitary dinner lady, Mrs Andrews, were on the far side of the playhouse, administering summary justice to the Year Sixes who were, once again, preventing access for the younger ones. I took a slow walk around the raised flower beds and wondered what they were doing in there. Running a poker school, possibly, although it was more likely just another of the wars of general possession that seemed to thread through the whole village, like gang warfare on a minor, and largely middle-class, scale. Lots of huffy garden fence moving and I suspected the local Planning Officer had Heavington written on his wall in black marker pen, with a 'Here Be Dragons' legend. We were close enough to the North York Moors National Park for the Buildings Regulations people to have to come out in pairs in unmarked cars to check up on illicit double-glazing installations. Ruthless politeness and exemplary manners stood in for machine guns and machetes and you lived to regret upsetting the Neighbourhood Watch, but it meant the village remained slightly feudalistic and impeccably picturesque.

Because of all this, strangers were rare, which was why I noticed the man standing near the front gate. Not *too* near, not hackle-raisingly near. Not near enough to the Year Ones who were pretending to be horses across the hopscotch square to make me step in, but near enough to draw my attention. He was young, fair-haired and he had one of those wide-featured faces, with a large mouth and eyes that smiled and always get called 'open'. It was wasted on me. I didn't trust any unknown adult within a hundred metres of my children. And I raised an eyebrow at a fair few known ones as well.

'Can I help you?'

The man came closer to the gate. 'I'm looking for the White Rose Retirement Home?' He gave me a grin. 'I'm thinking of reserving myself a place.'

I didn't smile back. 'Back along the lane and turn right. It's the big house on your left, you can't miss it. There's a name plate up on the gate.'

The man shivered. He was wearing a city raincoat, great at keeping out drizzle, but not much use against the east wind which battered against our neck of the woods like a bear trying to gain access to honey. 'Bit chilly, isn't it?'

I was wearing my fluffy grey jacket, the one that Rory said made me look like a pimp. I could only hope he didn't really know what a pimp was. The careers teacher at the local secondary was in for a shock when he met Rory. 'It's November.' Then I turned back to the playground. Sara Cowton was in charge of the whistle for the end of playtime this week, and she was draconian on timekeeping.

'My grandmother is moving in. To the White Rose,' the man said, behind me. 'And my brother and his wife are moving to the village. So my niece might be joining the school.'

I didn't turn around. 'Tell them to make an appointment to look round. Any time.'

I resisted the urge to look back over my shoulder to see if he went off in the direction of the White Rose, but the electrified feeling in my backpack of tension told me that he was still watching me, as I went round the side of the building to the children's entrance to wait for them to come in. It wasn't often these days that I had to deal with someone I didn't know. One of the joys of living in such a small place, everyone knew you and you knew everyone and even the driver that brought my weekly online groceries was the same small, semi-retired man every time. We lived in a little pocket of familiarity, and I liked it.

A brief flash of memory. University. My flat, on the sixth floor, full of people coming and going, laughter and parties. *Fun*. When had I last had fun? Oh, Irina had tried to get me to go to a concert with her, and I'd briefly entertained the idea and we'd enjoyed the planning, but in the end . . .

'Miss! Miss! Mister Immingham wants to know if we can start doing the Christmas play!' Timothy Grace and Imogen Wills bounced up in front of me. 'He's got the book and I want to be one of the mice!'

'The mice are the creatures that aren't doing anything, Imogen. It's not much of a part.' I turned, just once, before I rounded the corner, as they led the way into school. The man was still near the gate, looking as though he'd started to walk away but been interrupted. He wasn't looking at us, but down at the ground, still huddled in his town coat. I wondered why he'd come to the village instead of his brother who was moving here, but reasoned with myself he'd probably come to visit his grandmother and check the place out.

It would be nice, I thought, as Timothy and Imogen name-checked every character in *The Night Before Christmas* with varying degrees of desirability, to have some new starters. The school was dangerously low on numbers, and without our influx from the town, the villagers alone weren't enough to keep us open. Alan talked up our role as a community focus, the fact that the school buildings were used by lots of groups from the WI (who were critically low in membership themselves) to a local writing group (who, in contrast, seemed to gain members every week. If the WI set up a writing group I was fairly sure they could attain stasis) and, so far, he was managing to keep the Local Authority from closing us down. I'd got the impression that this Christmas play, providing, as it would, an entertainment for the White Rose

Home, was another of his measures to help keep us all from having to relocate. I could practically hear him, bouncing in to the council offices with his slightly stained tie flapping, announcing that Heavington School was such a public asset that we were within a whisker of a visit from royalty and a Lottery grant.

Oh dear. We really *were* going to have to do this Christmas play, weren't we?

We spent the afternoon casting the major parts, working on a little song for the sugar plums to sing as they danced about, and wondering how on earth we were going to get eight lots of reindeer costumes. Irina suggested two children each, like pantomime horses, but since nobody wanted to be the back-end, and Jonah North, Year Five's resident stand-up comedian, made up a mildly rude song about heads up bums, we decided to go with eight children wearing antlers and brown clothes.

I actually found myself admiring Jake during the casting session. He was firm but humorous, didn't react to Jonah's repeated chanting of 'floppy bums' with anything other than gentle exasperation, while Irina and I had to go and stand in the corridor for a moment until our composure returned. He had Years Five and Six sorted into 'those who want to act and those who would rather be offstage providing backing singers for the Sugar Plum Song', whilst I was still dealing with the Year Three wrangling about who wanted to be the child who stretched and yawned as they got into bed. There was a degree of stropping going on in the lower levels of Year Two, and I had the feeling that the stockings would not so much be 'hung by the chimney with care' as flung in the general direction of our mock chimney breast amid flouncing and competitive arm-folding, as I helped Irina assure everyone that, when it came to Christmas stockings, size was definitely not everything.

Outside the windows, the afternoon crept towards evening and leaves began to hit the glass with a regularity that spoke of another autumnal storm flying in. Our little enclave, snuggled in to the shoulders of the moors, was only twenty miles from the coast, and the weather came direct from Siberia, sometimes without a forwarding address. Farmers fetched the sheep down early here, and the cows came in to the yard, leaving the fields as stretched greyish expanses, broken by pools of rainwater which would be icing over any day now. We didn't have the worst weather in the world by any means, but in terms of unmitigated drabness, we had the edge. Days came late and left early, like reluctant office workers.

'Right,' Jake's briskness made me look away from the weather, and I noticed the gathering mothers restlessly circling the collecting ring of playground. Our casting session had taken most of the afternoon and it was nearly home time. 'Year Five and Six, go into the classroom and collect your things.'

'He is so masterful,' Irina whispered in my ear. 'I don't know why you don't like him, Lydia. He would make a very good man for you.'

'No thanks, he's not making anything for me, I've seen the clay dog he made at the beginning of term. Very unrealistic bits break off and the legs are different lengths.'

A moment of quiet and then Irina laughed, loudly enough to make her class stop twirling and stare at her. 'You need to get a life, Lydia.' And then she raised one hand in the air, which was her signal to her children to be quiet and listen to her, which they did, and she shepherded them back to their room to collect reading books, lunch boxes and small bags of damp knickers.

'Miss,' Rory sidled up to me as I led my class out of the hall. 'What's a nightcap? Mister Immingham said I need a nightcap. Dad has a nightcap every night and mum says he smells of booze, do I have to smell of booze?'

'No booze, Rory.' I said. 'We will talk about costumes another day, all right? Only your dad's here to collect you and you don't want to keep him waiting.' I looked into the playground at the tweed-jacketed figure of Rory's dad, a prematurely grey-haired man with the stoop of one who spends a lot of time with dough. I'd never noticed him smelling of booze, he normally smelled of flour and jam. But then, I'd learned to take a lot of what the kids said with a pinch of salt, otherwise I'd still believe that Aurora Grace lived in the old pig house and the baby had been flown in by jumbo jet. The Graces' mother was an author of children's books, and I think the children had got whimsicality by default.

'That all went better than I expected.' Jake was pulling on his coat. 'I thought there would be fights over who got to be Father Christmas, especially between the twins, but Timothy seems quite happy to let Oscar do it.'

I watched the children spilling out into the darkening air. They were all so full of life, full of potential, and I felt my past dragging at my heel like an anchor. Remembered how I'd been as a child; happy and trusting and energetic, so surrounded by the possibilities that the world had to offer. And now. With the weight of what had gone still unbalancing me. 'Timothy is a reindeer,' I said, only half my mind on the play. 'He said his mum wouldn't know it was him if he had a beard.'

'But he's quite happy for her not to recognise his brother?' Jake pulled his sleeves down. 'That figures.'

'And eight children isn't going to be too many?' Irina passed through, parcelling off her last child to its mother. 'We are not going to have eight beds on the stage, there isn't room.'

'We'll just lay them down under duvets or sleeping bags,' Jake said. 'As long as Father Christmas steps carefully and we can persuade Rory not to breakdance across the stage, we'll be fine. But they all want to stretch and make a performance of getting into bed, so it might take a while. We'll do a read-through next week, get some basic timings down.' He glanced at me and I was curiously aware that we were alone now. Outside all was bustle and chatter, but in this room, with the dark knocking at the windows, it felt very quiet. 'Are you sure you won't narrate?'

I just shook my head. 'Imogen will be far better than me.' To forestall any further questions, I began collecting my things together. I would rather have stayed, fiddled about in my room for a bit longer in the particular quiet that an empty school has, but I was a little bit worried that Jake might hang around and try to talk to me.

'It's an odd job that you do, for someone who doesn't want to be looked at.' Jake wasn't looking at me now. He'd got a carrier bag filled with what looked like school books and was checking the contents. 'You're the centre of attention in the classroom.'

Children don't judge. They see and they accept, and that's all there is to it. Their normal is, well, normal. Besides, what else can I do? 'I like teaching,' I said, and my voice was stiff and formal, my interview voice. Hadn't I answered this question before? 'It's all I ever wanted to do and I was in the middle of teacher training when . . . ' I stopped. He was looking at me now, focusing on me completely and I realised what made him such a good teacher. It felt as though a bomb could go off just outside the door and it wouldn't distract him. It was like having a laser pointer directly in my face, I couldn't move or look away. Along my back the tension wriggled and shifted but, to my surprise, it didn't rise up to strangle me. It grew and tugged, but then it settled. It didn't go, but neither did it threaten to pull me over backwards.

Jake kept looking. His dark eyes never left my face and I had the curious impression that he was somehow fishing out my secrets, luring them to the surface like trout from a deep pool. It didn't hurt as much as I expected. 'You — ' he began.

'Mister Immingham, my mum says can she talk to you about costumes for the play!' Timothy hurtled back in through the door and Jake switched off the tight focus on my face and turned with a grin. 'Course she can. I'm just coming, Tim. Tell her I'm on my way.' Then, as soon as the boy had launched himself back out into the playground, and whilst he was halfway out himself, he said, 'Are you all right?'

'Of course.' I stood up straight. 'Of course I am.'

'No 'of course' about it, y'know. You're allowed to be . . . ' and then he met my eye and my expression clearly told him that, however fit and toned his body may be, however broad his shoulders and attractive his dark hair and eyes, this was as far into my head as he went. 'Okay. Sorry. Yes, Tim, I'm coming!'

And then he was gone, out into the land of social chit-chat, of careless comments and throwaway observations, leaving me standing alone in the bright emptiness.

5

November 25th

It was late November and the weather was definitely drawing in now. Winter was tiptoeing ever closer, at the moment just brushing us with the edge of its cloak and crisping the early mornings, but soon the frosts would last all day and the sky would alternate from iron-grey to diamond-blue without any notable change in temperature. The hills stood out dramatically, as though they'd been cut out of card and stuck down onto the clouds that backed them and the air smelled of smoke and cold metal. At school my class had finished the constellation project just in time to start Christmas crafts — we were cutting snowflakes out of paper and studying how they were all different, as occasional sleet showers blew in and heaped white pellets in all the doorways.

Inside my cottage I'd got the wood-burner blazing, but because my walls were mostly metal, the heat dissipated quickly and I needed to wear thick socks and layers of fleece at all times. At night, ice sometimes formed on the insides of the windows and the water in the toilet had once frozen completely solid, which had been disconcerting, but I'd got used to winter here now. A change, yes, from the city, with its all-year-round temperatures, where heating systems got started in September as if to smooth out any change in the seasons. Only the flickering colours of the trees that lined the roads and the occasional wind skirling around the high buildings hinted of winter's approach there. Here, we were left in no doubt. Especially if, like me, you lived in a metal box with not much insulation.

This Saturday was the day of the much anticipated Christmas Fair. Anyone who made anything in Heavington, or grew anything or even just had a steady hand with colouring in, took a table in the school hall. There were stalls of knitted goods, cupcakes, occasionally knitted cupcakes, jigsaws, everything you could think of that might go in a bath or shower and the obligatory 'guess the weight of the Christmas cake' competition. The children had their own stall selling a mixture of indeterminate shapes covered in glitter, often with a robin on top, which they'd made in Art and balls covered in cotton wool, also usually with robin adornment, which were Christmas tree baubles. The main focus, though, was vast structures on wire netting frames, cast in plaster of Paris and painted to resemble tiny villages in the snow. It went without saying that these were also liberally dusted in glitter and scattered with robins, and marketed as 'table centrepieces,' which really only worked if you had a table the size of Belgium, but they sold these to fond parents and grandparents for one pound fifty pence a pop and everyone went home happy. We teachers bought up any leftover stock, and each year I'd been here my little tree had gained more and more random decorations, and my dining table resembled a relief map of the Alps done in glitter, but the children were delighted that their handiwork had sold and the money went towards next year's art supplies, so all was well. And it wasn't as though I had anywhere else to go on a grey Saturday in November, was it?

I wrapped up well. Although the school thermostat would be set somewhere between roasting and the furnaces of Hell, the walk would be cold, so I added a scarf, hat (that I'd bought at last year's sale and had been knitted by someone with more enthusiasm than skill with the Number 8's) and mittens before I fought the door open and stepped out into the wind. As I struggled to close the door behind me, a car drove past, slowly, headlights slicing the grey afternoon into organised segments. It passed me, went a few more yards, and then stopped, engine ticking, and a window slid down.

'Hello! We met outside the school a

couple of weeks ago! How are you?'

It was the blond-haired, friendly-faced man who'd asked the way to the White Rose. I pulled the door against the wind. For some reason I didn't want him to see inside my house. 'Hello,' I said, stiffly.

'Nice place you've got. Very quiet, shouldn't think you get much passing traffic.' He'd put his head out of the window to talk to me and the wind was chopping his hair into strips and trying to push it back into the car. 'It really is a lovely village.'

I couldn't really think of anything to say. General chit-chat wasn't something I had any practice in. My class tended to-wards focused comments or very detailed interrogations, they didn't really do small talk, and most adults wanted specific answers. So I just smiled and hoped he'd drive on.

'My grandmother loves the home. Says she has a nice view.' He was trying hard, I'd give him that, but there was really not much I could say in reply, was there? What did he want? Me to agree that, yes, his grandmother had a nice view? I'd only been in White Rose once, to take some flowers that had been delivered to school by mistake, and I was in no position to pass comment on the view, lovely though I was sure it was. So I settled for shrugging deeper into my coat and staring at the ground. It was marked with hoof-prints where the metalled road surface turned into bridleway and horses had to stand for their riders to open the hunting gate. The recent frost had set the prints hard in the mud, like handprints in clay, which reminded me that I had to get to the sale, before all the identifiable crafts sold out and I was left with the oddly-shaped gourds.

'So. Are you heading into the village? Can I give you a lift? It's a cold day.' The passenger door opened and a waft of mint-scented air puffed out, to be swept away on the breeze. 'I'd like to chat more about the school.'

I felt the hair on my neck prickle. It

could have been a warning, after all, never get in a car with a stranger was up there front and centre in the lessons about personal safety that we gave from Reception onwards. Or it could have been the chill wind getting between my scarf and my hat. But, either way, I didn't want him looking at me. 'No, thanks. I'm fine.'

'Are you sure?' And, again, that warm, mint-smelling air, that promised comfort. Wouldn't it be nicer to drive the half-mile to school than to slither and slide along the road edge, where the fallen leaves of autumn were crisping into a satin layer of slipperiness? But I'd have to get in and out of the car . . .

'Honestly, I'm fine.' I turned back to the door and pretended to be doing something fiddly with my key in the lock. In reality the door had locked as soon as it had swung shut, but he didn't know that and I definitely didn't want him to watch me start walking. Maybe I could go back inside, pretend I'd forgotten something? But as I scrabbled against the old Yale and twisted and turned the big key, he waved a hand and the car smoothly drove away towards the village, being swallowed into the grey light that was filtering down from the sky. I watched until the tail-lights turned the slight corner, and then set off myself, wondering why the man was here again and why his brother and family hadn't come to the school yet to introduce themselves. Surely they'd want their child to start at the beginning of the spring term, when we went back after the Christmas holidays? Unless they were waiting until summer to move, which, looking around me at the dew-dotted bare hedges that lined the road, would be sensible. Winter survival in Yorkshire was a learned knack, and if the family were moving from the south, then this area wouldn't start looking its best until May.

I meandered my way along the lane until I reached the school. Inside, the lights were on, laying bright tracks along the misty road for me to follow, until I reached the front door. Two members of the village committee charged me twenty pence to go into my own classroom, where I promptly walked into Jake, wearing a rugby shirt and different chinos. He looked like an off-duty sports commentator.

'Hello Lydia.'

We were buffeted by an assortment of over-excited, knee-level children — the local playgroup had come to visit Father Christmas in his grotto, or rather Alan, in an alarming beard and a red suit which fitted more snugly each passing year. When the initial tide had run down to a single three-year-old, he carried on. 'I was thinking we could do a dress rehearsal of the play next week?'

I nodded. 'We ought to start rehearsing, yes.'

He moved a little closer. 'Are you all right? You look a bit shaken up.'

I was just opening my mouth to deny anything was wrong, when I saw the car driver again. Now he was cruising around the stalls, picking up handmade soaps and engaging the stallholders in bright, animated chat. He'd got a holly wreath tucked under one arm and an expression of one who was enjoying themselves completely, which was so bizarrely out of place that it made my eyes widen. Anyone over four-feet-tall who was enjoying this overheated room full of random crafts had to be either starved of human company or on hard drugs. The under four-foot fraternity had Father Christmas and his £1 grotto presents to thank for their enthusiasm. I saw Sarah Cowton's mum, who helped in the kitchens at White Rose when she wasn't selling stamps, stop to say hello to him, and it reinforced my feeling of weirdness. She must have met him when he went to visit his grandmother, and the fact that someone else clearly found him pleasant enough to speak to made me wonder why I couldn't be nicer to him. Seriously, what *was* my problem, really? 'There's this man . . .'

I started, and then stopped myself. It was none of Jake's business. I could look after myself. 'No. I'm fine. Just came in to look for some Christmas presents.'

'Your family are mostly overseas aren't they?' Jake leaned himself against the wall, hands in the pockets of the chinos. He looked relaxed and comfortably at home, exchanging the odd smile with members of his class as they leaped from stall to stall, fuelled by pick'n'mix sweets and the excitement of seeing their Head Teacher with an unnecessary pillow down his front, handing out toys. 'You'll have a bit of a rush on to make last posting day.' The skin down my back twitched. 'How do you know my family are overseas?' My parents live in southern France and my sister is in Australia, so yes, fair enough. But I don't talk about them. Why would I? Who would care? Only me, that they aren't close enough to pop round to for tea and cake and a casual chat about life, but Martha works in environmental research and mum and dad like the heat, so it all seems sensible on the surface. And I told them I'm fine, I can manage, I don't need them. But I still slightly resented the fact that they believed me.

'Irina.'

Oh that girl was so dead. I narrowed my eyes in the direction of her classroom, but she wasn't here, she'd taken her children into York to meet a more believable Santa. I turned my suspicious gaze onto Jake. 'Have you two been discussing me?'

'No.' He gave me a grin. 'Why? Have you got hidden secrets?'

'If they weren't hidden, they wouldn't be secrets, would they? They'd be . . . whatever the opposite of secrets is. Facts. And no, I haven't, I just don't like being talked about.' Understatement. The thought of people talking about me, discussing me, made my flesh creep even more than the thought of someone walking behind me. It felt — *wrong*. Even more wrong to think of it being Irina, who I trusted, and Jake who . . . who . . . *who's the problem. The reason you can't even think about another man.*

'Okay.' And he nodded his head, as though he was filing my observation away for later study. 'Well, don't worry, she didn't give away any of your non-secrets, we were just talking generally about Christmas plans. Are you staying in the village this year?'

'I stay at home, yes.'

'I expect your hut is very Christmassy.' The twitch to his lips stopped the sudden offence I was about to take.

'Yes. For a hovel it's very seasonal. Now, I'd better get on, all the best lumps of plaster will be gone if I don't get moving.'

Jake looked over at the school stall, where Oscar Grace was carefully counting change out to Mrs Wilkinson, who had just bought a small hunk of tree liberally sprinkled with fake snow, glitter and a dusting of robins. 'I think that ship may have sailed,' he said quietly. 'If you get the three decorations in that box, I'll take the rest. Just watch out for the weight of the damn things. I swear, next year we're doing cards. Small ones.'

'I'll do my best.' I gave him an answering smile, because I knew him well enough now to know that the children's enthusiasm for plaster of Paris and plastic robins would win him round again next year. Designing a school Christmas card was nowhere on the excitement scale, when you could be making your own winter wonderland, and the fact we had to start them in October so the plaster had chance to dry out, just extended the season of hysterical exhilaration.

'Go on then.' Jake gave my shoulder the merest hint of a push and the touch of his hand, even through my big coat, made me realise that it had been a long time since anyone had made physical contact with me. I was always so careful. So separate. 'Before I change my mind and leave you with all of it.'

'You wouldn't dare. After all, I live in a hut, remember? Too many 'table decorations' and the foundations would give way. I'd fall into a huge Christmassy hole and nobody would find me for six weeks, I'd be living on glitter and glue.' And then I had to turn away before my face gave away what my words nearly had. That fear. Fear of something happening and nobody noticing, nobody coming to look for me until it was too late, and the horror almost unbalanced me. It sent me across the room faster than I would normally go, and I ended up lurching into the back of the blond-haired smiling man, who turned around as I arrived and nearly had me smeared across his front.

'Hello again! We must stop meeting like this!' He took my arm to steady me, and dropped the holly wreath he'd been holding. 'It's Lydia, isn't it? Forgive me, I heard you in conversation with your friend . . . my name's Gareth. Gareth Graham. That's my full name, it's not like a hyphenated first name, blame my parents. How are you?'

I thought for a moment he was going to shake my hand, but he just juggled all his purchases and then slowly bent to pick up the wreath. I didn't want to answer his question as to how I was. He was friendly and chatty and personable, but I just didn't. And, when I looked up and across the crowded hall, Jake was watching me with an eyebrow raised, which made me feel even more uncomfortable. 'I'm . . . yes, I'm fine. Please excuse me, I need to have a word with one of my pupils.'

Oscar Grace was an unlikely conversational saviour, but he would have to do, and I headed for the school stall with an alacrity that I wasn't sure was necessary. Gareth Graham might be a bit omnipresent, but in a village this size so was everyone else. You couldn't escape the same half-dozen people. Just popping into the Post Office for a stamp was fraught with fending off questions about the National Curriculum and school league tables, or tales of how the village school used to be one room next to the church, with liberal caning — and, apparently, none the worse for it. So if the same faces popping up in unlikely circumstances was perfectly normal, why was this man's recurrence making me nervous?

'I'll have these three decorations please, Oscar.' I picked up the box. 'One pound fifty pence each'.

Oscar's lips moved as he worked out my bill. Then, 'is that man your boyfriend, Miss?'

I sighed. The children had what I considered to be an unhealthy fascination with our lives outside the school. So far they'd had me practically married to every single man in the village, including Mrs Wilkinson's nephew, who was fifty and lived with his horses in an old barn. I'd once had a conversation with him over a gate, and the children were having a collection for our wedding before I got back into class.

'No. He's a man whose grandmother has come to live at the White Rose. He comes to visit her, I think.'

'He likes you though.' Oscar took my five pound note and put it in the butter tub that was holding the takings. I was pleased to see that there were a good number of fivers and tenners in there already. Tables around the village would be groaning in anticipation. 'He's looking at you all the time.'

I resisted the urge to check. 'That's as maybe but he's not my boyfriend.'

'Mister Immingham likes you too. He said, he said he likes you.'

I couldn't even begin to imagine how the topic of Jake liking me might crop up with a bunch of ten-year-olds, so I didn't try. Sometimes the children would fire questions that sounded like a Mastermind round on LSD, you got used to it.

'Who's that man's grandma?' Oscar brought me back from sliding into a little bit of a Jake-related dream. 'My dad works at the White Rose sometimes, he says some of the ladies are old fusspots. Old. Fusspots,' he repeated, as though he liked the sound of the words. Oscar had a good dose of his author mother's genes.

'Not sure. Anyway, I'd better get going home. We're going to try a dress rehearsal of the play on Monday, Oscar, so maybe you'd like to read through the book again over the weekend. And I'll ask Mr Roberts if we can borrow his beard for you,' I added in a conspiratorial tone, just in case any of the little children thought that Father Christmas really was hiding out in the small cleaning cupboard, unconvincingly decked out in tinsel. The under-fives lacked the critical faculty to wonder why a man with the whole of the Arctic Circle at his disposal would hang around with an industrial hoover and the smell of Domestos. The magic of Christmas, I suppose.

I stared around for a moment. At the classroom and school hall, festooned with limp crepe paper and silver foil stars. At the big tree that I knew Alan would have spent the morning wrestling into place and decorating, probably co-opting Mrs Andrews in to help. At the excited faces of the children, comparing their early presents from Father

Christmas or trying to get the lids off tiny pots of Play-Doh. The grey light of the coming night starting to curtain the windows from outside, making this little bright world seem even more self-contained and filled with potential.

I hated myself for seeing the rips in the paper chains and the dust on the stars. Hated that I couldn't just let myself go and throw myself into the almost tangible anticipation. I knew why I couldn't feel the magic, because I was too busy feeling sorry for myself, but somehow I just couldn't stop.

'Deep in thought?' It was Gareth Graham. Smiling blue eyes and such an appealing grin. It made me feel even worse about not getting the Christmas spirit. 'Christmas can be hard work, can't it?' He said it almost as though he could read what I felt, but then, it was probably obvious from my expression. 'Any chance I could offer you a cup of tea? I passed a tea shop on the way here, and it would be great to be able to pick your brains about the locality. For my brother, I mean, he can't get up here for a while so I'm scoping the place out for him and his family.'

I glanced across the room. Jake was talking to Mrs Wilkinson, who had practically cleared most of the stalls. She had four grown-up children and they had provided her with enough grandchildren that, for her, Christmas shopping had to start in August. She used the school fair to mop up those last presents and her bag bulged with miniature iced cakes and handmade soaps. If it had been me, I'd have wrapped them separately, but no doubt she knew what she was doing.

Jake met my eye across the room and nodded. Then he looked at the big box tucked under my arm, grinned and gave me a sudden wink that sent me lurching, flustered and warm, towards the door, where Gareth was, yet again, waiting. 'I ought to get home,' I said, but my words were weak. Half of me wanted to go home, to light the fire and sit wrapped in fleeces, watching repeats of *Murder She Wrote* and marking last week's homework. But the other half of me, the half that could feel the press of Christmas and the longing to get caught up in it all, wanted to sit somewhere steamy and eat mince pies. And, in this crazily busy room, with Jake chatting to a parent and laughing, I felt an echoing loneliness. Could it really be so bad to just sit and talk to someone? And if I couldn't talk, really *talk*, to the man I wanted to talk to, then — why not? 'But I suppose a quick cup of tea would be nice. And you can ask me anything about the village.'

'Oh, I will.' Gareth held the door open for me. 'And I understand there's a Christmas play in the offing? That sounds interesting.'

I found myself telling him about *The Night Before Christmas*, the casting and the costume dilemmas, almost as though I was trying to entertain him on the walk to the tea shop. And I wasn't sure why, because his closeness still made that tension tickle between my shoulder blades, despite his floppy hair and his cheeky grin. I think it was something to do with the way he kept using my name, like it was a new toy that he was trying out to see if the wheels would stay on. It made me uncomfortable.

'So, Lydia.' We sat down at a table. Mrs Scott began making a pot of tea behind the counter, widening her eyes at me in question at the sight of Gareth. I just shrugged. He might be a bit over the top, but a scone is a scone and I was tired of my own cooking. 'What brought you here to teach in this little school?'

'I like it.'

'That's not what I asked.' He leaned a little closer across the melamine, steam from the teapot wobbling the outline of his face. 'What I mean is, what's a nice girl like you doing in a place like this?'

I blinked.

'Sorry, sorry, too much of a cliché? I just, well. You know.' He looked down at his hands. They were very fine-boned and looked young, like a child's hands. Like hands that had never done anything. 'Anyway.'

'Is your grandmother still enjoying the White Rose?' I blurted out, then lifted my teacup to prevent my mouth from sabotaging the conversation any further. The thin china fizzled against my upper lip with the heat of the tea, and I forced down the inner cynic, who was trying to tell me that Gareth was chatting me up, with a mouthful of scone.

'Er. Yes. Yes, thank you, she is.' He looked confused for a moment, and started fiddling with the sugar lumps. 'And my brother is very much looking forward to moving here. How many children do you teach?'

I gave him a potted history of the school as I knew it. Told him that we'd got thirty-four children in total, that the school might be under threat if we didn't increase our numbers, that most of the children came in from beyond the village. And all the while it got darker outside, the windows grew steamier and we were the only customers. It was like being in a black and white film. I half expected a steam train to whistle outside and a lot of people wearing gabardine and hats to come in.

Eventually I stopped talking and ate the last of my scone. Gareth was smiling at me again. It was the sort of smile that says 'I haven't heard a word you've been saying, because I've been too busy watching your mouth move,' and I felt that small icy finger poke my spine again. *Why am I even here? Because even tea with a serial killer is better than sitting alone? That's complete bollocks ... and even worse, Lydia, you are lying to yourself, because you know exactly why you came here. You wanted Jake to see you walk off with another man. You wanted, in some juvenile, Year Four way, to make him jealous. Poor Jake, who you can barely stand to have a conversation with — because you fancy him, and you know he will never want you, so you are distancing yourself as fast as you can.*

'I'm sorry, Gareth, but I have to go.' I stood up, hoping that he wouldn't think that the blush was because of him. 'I've got marking to do, and some reindeer antlers to sew on before Monday.'

He stood up too. 'Then please let me give you a lift home. It's dark and that road isn't very safe to walk along. I mean, it must be slippery and you . . . ' he stopped. Flipped his glance down to the floor and then back to my face. 'It must be difficult,' he said.

'I will be fine.' I was glad to hear that my voice sounded more definite than I felt. But then, it was used to saying things I didn't really mean. To keeping things at bay. 'Thank you.'

'Oh, but . . . '

'Really. Why don't you pop in and see your grandmother? You could take her the holly wreath, I'm sure she'd like it to put up on her door.' I'd got my 'teacher' tone on, I could hear it myself.

That no-nonsense, we-are-going-to-do-as-I-say, voice that I usually reserved for my class when they got hyped up about something. Last time it had been when a small dog got loose in the playground and they'd all clustered by the window to watch its owner attempting to catch it. It had been amusing for three minutes, but then I'd had to get back to our World Map, and I'd had to wheel no-nonsense out for a good ten minutes before they'd started to concentrate again. Nathan had had to go and sit in Alan's office for the rest of the morning, he didn't deal well with unexpected events.

'I could. I suppose.' There was a distinct Year Four sulky tone to Gareth's voice now. 'But can I see you again sometime?'

'Less than a hundred people live in Heavington. You couldn't miss me if you had your eyes closed and your arms strapped down.' The clinging feeling that tightened my skin was guilt now, rather than suspicion, and the guilt was making me sharp. Did Gareth think I wanted him to date me? Or even that I was available to date? And all the time the creeping knowledge that I was only here because I couldn't be with Jake Immingham and his strong shoulders, unruly hair and dark eyes, tainted the aftertaste of my delicious fruit scone with bitterness.

My own fault, of course. My own catch-22. I was rude to Jake because I liked him but I knew he would never want me, and the rudeness just proved to him that I wasn't very nice, and therefore not the kind of woman he would ever want to be with. And so it circled. And so, I stayed alone. Because alone is better than pitied, alone is better than used as a warning — 'things might be tough, but at least you aren't Lydia.' To be seen as noble and self-disregarding, because you went out with someone like *me*. God, sometimes I was so self-pitying it even made me feel sick.

Gareth smiled that young, untroubled smile again. 'I suppose I can't,' he said, cheerfully. 'Well, if you're sure you're all right to get home, I shall, as they say, see you around.'

I let him leave first by a wide margin. I wanted to make sure that he wasn't sitting outside in his car, waiting for me. Turning down a lift home would have been so much harder if he'd driven up alongside me, I would have started to look churlish rather than independent, and, after all, I didn't want to alienate him totally. He might advise his brother against our school, and while one more child wasn't going to cause the Local Authority to admit that we were totally safe, it would be one more on the roll and one more lot of money in the school coffers. Once I considered it ought to be safe, I took my teacup and plate up to the counter, to save Mrs Scott the trip, and headed out into the dark of the winter afternoon.

There was nothing scary about Heavington in the dark, despite the lack of streetlights. The moon was full enough, even strained through the net of tree branches, that it lit the way back to my house. I set out past the little square of houses that formed the main village street, down the lane past the school. All the lights were out now and the cars had all gone. Mrs Wilkinson would have left most of the tidying up to do tomorrow, and gone home to watch the football. She'd be sitting there now, in the tiny cottage at the back of the playground, wrapping Christmas presents in front of the fire and yelling abuse at Chelsea when they scored, I could see the light on in her living room window from here.

Further down the lane lay the Queen Anne Manor House. White Rose as it was now known. Of course, it didn't front onto the lane like the plebeian dwellings of the rest of the village, it lay down the end of its driveway, which curled like a cat's tail around the building. Huge cedar trees bulked between it and the road, dark looming things in the night, on either side of the iron double gates, which stood open as

I passed, but I couldn't see any cars. Didn't know whether Gareth really had gone to visit his grandmother, and I wasn't going to toddle down that loose gravelled drive to find out.

A few squares of light at some upstairs windows spoke of residents going about their business in their little self-contained flatlets, and the blaze and flicker from downstairs showed that the TV lounge was occupied too. I could just see the range of steps which led up to the front door, illuminated by a string of coloured lights which had been woven between the railings. They swung slightly in the breeze, but there was no sign of any activity other than that.

I walked on back to my home. The glow from White Rose was just visible from my doorway and it helped to see it and to know that there were other people out there in the world. Otherwise the old village hall was isolated from all other buildings, and on some days when there was no school, the only people I saw were the bobbing heads of riders as they trotted past or opened the bridle path gate. They usually had their attention on their horses, but occasionally one would glance my way, make eye contact and then ride off, leaving me feeling even lonelier for the brief interaction.

The hall was still warm, but I lit the woodburner again anyway, more for the company of the flickering flame than anything else. Then I sat and listened to the owls on the roof, the steady drip of damp from the trees in the hedgerow, the crackle of the fire. After the noise and bustle of the Christmas Fair it should have been soothing, but today it only highlighted how alone I was out here, in a self-imposed isolation that I thought I enjoyed, but that I was increasingly coming to see as an extended sulk. The box of table decorations sat accusingly beside me with the smell of glue and plaster radiating off it as the warmth grew. It positively shouted that Christmas shouldn't be confined like this, it should be allowed to fill the whole house, but I couldn't bring myself to unpack it. I should have dotted the decorations around on the shelves, used them to show how I was getting in the Christmas spirit, along with my tasteful collections of pine cones and driftwood and artfully knitted hangings, but I couldn't.

Today's encounter with Gareth, his eagerness to chat and try to get to know me, had thrown up so many memories. So many doubts. So much regret. Because my life couldn't be the way I wanted it, would *never* be the life I had hoped for and half-planned, during those years of university and teacher training. Oh, I could have a sort-of life, of course I could, I wasn't *dead*. But so much had been lost, and now ... I looked around me. Now I should be counting my blessings instead of pining for a man I couldn't have and feeling creeped out by the man who showed any sign of wanting me.

I allowed myself an obligatory five-minute wallow, then blew my nose sharply and started on the pile of books I had to mark.

6

'No, no, Jocasta, it's fine!' I tried my best soothing voice, but Jocasta would not be placated.

'I *can't* go to bed in my school uniform! Mummy says it's not allowed.'

I sighed and tried to ignore Irina digging me in the ribs with her elbow. 'Look. It's just a dress rehearsal, you don't have to ... Rory! Rory, calm down!'

Jocasta wasn't the only one to have forgotten her costume, and a kind of communal despondency was breaking out.

'Do we have to brush our teeth? Only we have to at home. Miss, miss, where do we brush our teeth?'

Jake threw me a look over the heads of our cast. Along with despondency, it now looked as though we had an out-break of literalism. 'Alex, it's a play. Not real life. Yes, you have to brush your teeth in real life but — you don't see Captain America brush his teeth, do you?'

Alex frowned. 'But you don't see Captain America put his pyjamas on either,' he said, reasonably. 'So, so, maybe Captain America never goes to bed!'

'Don't be stupid.' Rory bounced past, wiggling the hem of his nightshirt as though he was about to break into a Folies Bergère routine. 'You don't see him weeing either, and he must, otherwise he'd burst.'

I heard Jake's intake of breath. Irina had her head in her hands now. 'Okay,' Jake said, slowly. 'Maybe we should move on to the reindeer. Rory, let's take it from 'went to the window and threw up the sash', shall we?'

Irina and I cleared the stage and Rory positioned himself at the cardboard win-dow. 'Ready!' he said, cheerfully and unnecessarily.

'*Away to the window I flew like a flash.*'

'Can you speak up a bit, please, Imogen?'

'*Away to the window I flew like a flash,*' Imogen said again, at exactly the same, tiny, volume.

'A bit more.'

Imogen repeated the line twice more, with no notable increase in noise. Jake waved a hand and Rory, who obviously hadn't heard a word of the narration, 'threw up the sash' with such force that our cardboard frame tore at the top and the 'window' shot across the stage and hit one of the reindeer. As the reindeers' antlers flopped about on their headbands and looked more like ears, the sight of one of them dashing across the stage to complain about the affront to his dignity on being smacked with a paper window reduced Irina and I nearly to tears of helpless laughter. This first dress rehearsal was not going well.

By the end of the read-through,

several of the sugar plums were bored and wandering about, Imogen had dropped to a whisper, Rory was dancing around in his nightshirt singing 'Despacito' with made-up words, and Jake, Irina and I were stretching our tethers about as far as they would go.

'Remind me again who said this was a good idea?' Jake cued up Oscar and his sleigh for the final scene again, trying to stop the Grace twins from shoving each other, whilst the flopping effect of the antlers was driving Irina and I into tired hysterics as we marshalled the remainder of the cast to the back of the makeshift stage to wave at Father Christmas as he rode past at the front.

'Alan,' Irina and I said together.

'Any chance we can ply the White Rose crew with whisky so they don't notice the chaos?' Jake stood back. 'And you two aren't helping. You're not supposed to giggle like loons all the time.'

'Sorry. It's the antlers,' I said, trying

to hide my sniggering from the children. 'They look . . . well . . . '

'They are looking like floppy willies,' Irina whispered, which set me off again, and Jake threw his hands in the air.

'Okay everyone, I think that's enough rehearsing for today. Get changed and then back to class, all of you.'

Irina went to help the sugar plums change out of their costumes. The rest of the children piled through into Jake's classroom, which we'd used as a changing room whilst we rehearsed in the hall, amid much chatter and laughter. We were only a week from the end of term, and timings meant that, this year, it fell two days before Christmas Eve, so excitement and anticipation were running through the school like an electrical charge. The children were hyped and silly and keeping them quiet and calm enough to do any work was a full-time job, never mind actually teaching them anything. We'd taken to lots of outdoor work, nature walks and drawing and generally trying to give them fresh air and exercise to damp down the hysteria. The fact that snow was forecast, and odds were being given on a white Christmas, wasn't helping one little bit, because my class would run to the window at every drop of precipitation, to check whether it had started to snow yet.

We couldn't break up soon enough.

'Nice to see you laughing,' Jake said, as we waited for our respective charges. 'You're always so serious, Lydia.'

It was a pleasant exchange, just chit-chat. But the fact that it was Jake meant I had to forestall any pleasantness. Couldn't bear him being nice to me, because it gave me hope that I had no right to have. No *reason* to have. It would have been so much easier if he'd been horrible.

'I laugh a lot. Just not when you're around,' I replied.

'Fair enough.' A moment's silence. 'So, how's it going with that bloke you left the Fair with, the other week? I've not seen him around before, must be a newcomer?'

The question surprised me. I didn't think he'd even noticed me leave the fair. Why would he? 'Oh, I don't know him. He's scoping out the school for his brother, and his grandmother has just moved into the White Rose, so he comes to visit her. We just keep running into each other.' I kept my eyes on the cupboard behind Jake's head. Didn't want him to think I was actually looking at the way he was watching my face. Couldn't bear to see his gaze flick downwards, as people's always did. Looking. Wondering. Because I didn't want Jake to be like everyone else. Knew he would be, of course, he was just a man, just another man; the way I secretly felt about him didn't stop that. I shouldn't put him on a pedestal, no matter how covertly. *He was just a man*. I kept telling myself that.

But even more secretly, I couldn't believe it. He was just so nice! Good-looking, a great teacher, kind . . . which was why I had to keep my distance. Be cold and unfriendly to him. 'Any particular reason you want to know?'

'Er, no. Just an idle wonder, and Mrs Scott mentioned it to Mrs Wilkinson who mentioned it to me, so . . . '

Of course, village gossip. I'd been the subject of much of it when I'd first come to Heavington, but my years of doing absolutely nothing noteworthy had dulled the communal interest. 'I was just telling him about the school, and our league table status.'

'Wow. Riveting stuff.' He put his hands in his pockets and sort of stuck his elbows out, as though mentally searching for another topic of conversation. 'So. What are you doing for Christmas this year? Looks like we might have snow.'

'So the forecast says.'

'You are hard work, Lydia. I'm just chatting, all right?' There was something — anger? Amusement? — in his eyes. 'You don't have to be so snippy all the time.'

Then I did something I rarely do, something I can't afford to let myself do. I snapped. 'Yes, I do. Because, you know something? Snow isn't pretty for me. It's not some lovely festive decoration that makes the village look clean and Christmassy, it's something that stops me leaving my house. And yes, I do have to be snippy, because I'm sick of people pitying me, feeling sorry for me talking to me out of politeness or wanting to ask 'what happened to you?' Wanting the dirt, wanting all the inside information! And, do you know something else? I'm fed up with being the one that everyone gossips about behind my back!'

Tears I hadn't even been aware were building were starting to slide down my cheeks and I sniffed loudly, turned and walked as fast as I could out of the hall and down to the little teachers' room at the end of the corridor. For a few moments I didn't care that my class wouldn't know where I'd gone, all I wanted was two minutes to regain my composure. To slip back into the ice-maiden persona that I'd cultivated and hung on to so hard that my fingers ached.

Footsteps in the passageway and Jake came through the door. 'I'm taking you home.'

'I can't go home!'

'Yes, you can. It's only half an hour until school is over, Jackie has your class and Alan is minding mine. I've told them you've been taken ill. It's all done, Lydia, please, just let me take you home.'

I took a deep breath. 'This is my life.'

'Being like this?' Jake came over and held out my coat. 'Or the school?'

A snorty laugh escaped. 'Both.'

'Look. Teaching is stressful, we both know that. It's high pressure and it doesn't let up, even in this sort of environment.' He waved a hand to encompass the whole school. 'I deal with it by not letting it get to me. I came into teaching after training to be an engineer, you know.' He dropped out of his stern tone and became more conversational. 'All my family are engineers. I mean high-powered, design and technology, bells and whistles stuff.' He helped me into my coat almost without me realising he was doing it. 'And it took a while to dawn on me that, just because my mum and dad and my brother are all engineers, *I* didn't have to be one. I wasn't born under the star sign Dyson. It's not predetermined.'

He opened the side door and let us out into the cold air. The day had been bright but the sun was setting and the air had crisped around the edges. The brown ghosts of fallen leaves were stuck to the pavement like a mosaic and the low sun slanted down through the hedges, making the hawthorn berries and rose hips that were hanging on despite hungry birds glow like little lanterns.

'So, that's me.' Jake fell into step beside me as we headed down the lane. 'What about you?'

I shrugged. 'Nothing to know.'

He turned to look at me but I kept my eyes on the ground. I could see the side of his face out of the corner of my eye and there was a half-smile on his mouth. 'Really? That little outburst earlier says different.'

But I'd got it under control now. And, nice as it was walking along the lane with Jake with the setting sun in our faces and the rooks calling themselves home over our heads in a ragged cloud, my guard was back up. 'Yes. Sorry about that. I think I'm just tired. It's been a long term, and we seem to have the Christmas play from hell on our hands. It all got a bit much.'

We walked along in relative silence for a bit. We weren't talking, but the cacophony of nature around us filled in any conversational gap. Over at the farm, the cows in the yard were mooing to be let into the parlour for milking, away in a field a tractor chugged determinedly back and forth and the race to the roost had begun for the small birds, who were fighting for prime position in the hedges. At the entrance to the White Rose, I stopped.

'Thanks for walking me back. I'll be fine from here.'

'Are you sure? I'd like to see you all the way to your door, really.' He was looking ahead now, as though he could visually project us down the road. Then he flicked a quick glance my way. 'To make sure you're all right.'

'I am fine.' And I sounded determined. Hard. 'I'll see you at school tomorrow. Please thank Jackie for minding the class,' and I started to walk on ahead.

'Lydia!' His voice sounded stretched, although he wasn't that far behind me. 'I'm sorry. But I don't know how to play this. I try to treat you like everyone else, but, you know something? Being disabled does *not* entitle you to be a complete dick!'

I stopped. '*What?*'

'Okay, yes, and now I come to think about it, that came out a lot more confrontational than I was intending, but it's true. I'm sure you have your reasons and that it's second nature to you and all that, but.' A deep breath. 'Yep, sorry. You're still coming over like a dick.'

Now I started to walk again. *What else did you expect, Lydia? Of course he's just like all the others, of course he is? Being all rugged and muscular and cute and good with kids doesn't stop him from basically being just the same as everyone else, does it? Unable to see, unable to understand.* 'I'll see you tomorrow.' The words were so stiff they could have been in a mortuary.

'Lydia, I'm . . . '

I didn't even slow down now. My eyes were focused on the warm safety of my house, there, at the end of the lane, although it was blurry through the tears that kept on forcing their way down my face. *How dare he? How DARE he call me a 'dick'? I had to keep people at a distance, that was all, stop them getting close, stop the pity and the questions*

— why could he not see that?

'Hello, dear.' The voice, from the top of the wall of the White Rose, made me lose my balance and I had to stop and catch at the brickwork so as not to fall. A half-glance over my shoulder reassured me that Jake had gone and wouldn't have seen my momentary lapse, and a full glance upwards revealed an elderly lady, either levitating or up a ladder. She was leaning her elbows on the coping stones of the wall and wielding a large pair of shears, which she waved at me. 'Ivy,' she said.

'Hello, Ivy.' The words were a bit breathless as my heart was hammering too fast for me to be able to draw the air in.

'Oh, no, that's not my name. I'm Marguerite. I'm cutting back the ivy, that's what I meant. It's a real nuisance on the brickwork you see. You're that young teacher from the school, aren't you?'

Now I knew how Alice felt, talking to the caterpillar on his mushroom, and

I'd be able to read that section from *Alice's Adventures in Wonderland* to my class with a lot more conviction. It was just so ridiculous, addressing what appeared to be a floating head. Even if the caterpillar hadn't had carefully cut grey hair and a pair of glasses which seemed to be attached to a fluorescent green string, and Lewis Carroll had remained quiet on the subject of the cloud of *Poison* which was evident to my nose even at some distance.

'I teach at the school, yes.'

'Excellent.' The shears clattered. 'We are all so looking forward to the Christmas play! Most exciting thing most of us will have been to since they took us to that exhibition in York and Brian lost his trousers. And it's so nice to have something *Christmassy* to look forward to, if you see what I mean, because, honestly, most of it is just a nice dinner and a long nap. It's such fun to watch the children getting over-excited and know that it's not going to be you woken up at four in the morning to see them open their presents.' She settled her elbows more comfortably on the wall.

'What are you standing on?'

'Ladder,' she replied. 'Oh, don't worry, I've done all my Health and Safety stuff. Brian's holding it for me down the bottom. Aren't you, Brian!' she called.

A voice, muffled by distance, brickwork and ivy floated back. It sounded affirmative.

'Don't you have a gardener?'

'Oh yes. But it's nice to have a purpose sometimes. Life in here can get a bit . . . ' She glanced up and down the road and lowered her voice, as though the place was run by the Stasi. 'Samey. Boring. I like the odd challenge. Don't I, Brian?'

'Arfnurnurfnur'.

I had no idea what that was supposed to be.

'Yes, thought you must be a teacher. A couple of the residents have got grandchildren at the school, they've mentioned you. Great grandchildren, I think, in Ruby's case. Anyway, they talk about you.' A shrewd look. 'Are you the Polish one or have you only got one leg?'

I opened my mouth. Nothing came out.

'You don't sound Polish, so I suppose you're the other one. Miss . . . Knight, is it? Never was good with names.'

'ArfnurnurFURnur.' It sounded as though Brian seconded that.

'Lydia Knight, yes.'

'Can't shake hands, up a ladder.' Marguerite looked down. 'We had a meeting, you know. About the school.'

Ninety per cent of me wanted to keep walking. To get home and get out of my teaching clothes, into my loose, comfortable, slobbing about wear. I was tired and Jake's words kept echoing around in my head with just the tiniest hint of question — *was he right? Was I, in his words, 'being a dick'? Keeping people at a distance not to protect myself but because I couldn't be bothered to make the effort to be nice?*

— and then the ten per cent of me that knew we needed the White Rose on our side to help keep the school open, should it come to it, cut in.

'What sort of a meeting? I mean, we don't really have much of a connection, do we?'

'That's why we had the meeting. It seems ridiculous, the school over there and you all understaffed and over-worked and everything, and here's us, in here, underworked and overstaffed, and, to be honest, most of us are bored out of our trees. We thought we could do some sort of exchange visits. If you were agreeable, you see.' The shears clipped at something, as though to punctuate her point.

'Exchange visits?' I asked, weakly.

'Yes. We thought, some of us could come into school and maybe listen to the young ones read, teach them some of the old crafts — we've got Eleanor who used to make lace, and Poppy is a demon with the knitting, and maybe you could bring some of them over here

110

now and then? Listen to some of the older ones rambling on about the War, that sort of thing?'

Maybe next year we could get the children to make lace or knit things for the stall . . . my arm ached with a kind of residual memory of carrying the box of plaster ornaments. *And we've got a topic coming up on World War Two — having an actual living resource on our doorstep would be a huge bonus.* 'That sounds like an amazing idea. The children would love it.' As would OFSTED.

'And it can get a bit lonely in here too.' Marguerite ran a thumb along the shears. 'I mean, I have Brian . . . '

'Fnurnur.'

' . . . but so many of the others are spending more and more time in their rooms, it's quite worrying. It's one of the downsides to being old, feeling a bit redundant. Not useful any more, and it makes some of us a wee bit lonely. That's why I thought of the school, we might not be any good at a lot of things, but we can help the next generation. You have to be — now, what's the word? Like yoghurt. Proactive, that's it. You have to be proactive. Otherwise, what's the point? 'Died a lonely old biddy' isn't much of an epitaph, now, is it?'

'Quite.' Her words made me feel a small stab of guilt. Self-imposed isolation because of feeling that there was so much you couldn't do, that was me to a T. 'I'll mention it to Alan on Monday, but I think it sounds like a wonderful idea, twinning White Rose with the school.' I looked up at the sky. 'We ought to get on, it looks like snow. I have to get home and you don't want to be up a ladder in a blizzard.'

'Oh. Of course, yes. I'm sorry, I do go on a bit sometimes.'

'FnurNURfnur.'

'It's just that I don't see many new faces, it's harder for those with limited mobility, you see. Another reason that we're looking forward to your Christmas play, a chance to see other people from the village. Oh, there's a few have family here, but not all of us, and it's just pleasant.'

'You must get new residents though, from time to time. Haven't you just got someone new? A lady whose family are thinking of moving here?' Gareth Graham and his grandmother must be the centre of attention if new faces were hard to come by. I could just see him doing his super-friendly smile to the ladies in here, I'd bet that at least half of them would be in love with him. And the other half would have him doing odd jobs around the place, given half an hour.

Marguerite frowned. 'I don't think so.' She looked down towards the base of her ladder. 'Brian, have we had anyone new in?'

'Fnurfnurfnur.'

'Not her, she's been here ages. Who was the last one in? Oh, yes, Gerald. But he's not a grandmother though, evidently.' She looked back over the wall at me. 'No, no new faces for a

113

couple of years. So, again, it would be lovely to have the children coming and going a little around the old place. And I know it's a little late for this year, but perhaps, next year, might you, perhaps, need a hand with any of the costumes? So many of us in here are a dab hand with the needle, you know. Although,' and her face went a bit wobbly as she glanced down, presumably at Brian, 'the arthritis has put a stop to so much, for a lot of people.'

My brain did a kind of double-take. 'Nobody new at all?'

'Only Gerald, and he's been here since, what spring 2015? I know it was spring, we'd just got the first daffs up and he ran over them in his chair. Never liked the man after that, but he does have good whisky.' Marguerite stared dreamily across over my head into the field beyond the lane, as though memories of distant days were frolicking over the rough ploughed land.

'Fnurnur.'

'I know you don't, but we have to

make allowances.'

'Someone who might be visited by a youngish man? Blond hair? Very smiley?'

'Oh, that sounds like Gary! No, dear, Gary is the new handyman, who comes in to fix things. He's been in a couple of times lately. Fixed Poppy's door a while back, and he was here a week or so ago to do something to the roof.'

So Gareth Graham was a liar. No grandmother in the White Rose. And, presumably, by extension, no family thinking of moving to the village either. I gritted my teeth. 'I shall put your suggestion to Alan tomorrow, when I get in to school.' And the sudden memory of the reindeer antlers flopping about on their headbands came to me. 'And it would be wonderful to have some help with costumes for next time around.'

'That would be lovely. It would be so nice to feel that we had something we could help with. Give us an investment in watching, if you see what I mean.'

Oh dear Lord, that would mean we'd

have to do another play next year. I'd practically promised, hadn't I? Maybe I could get a job somewhere on an isolated island before then. Wasn't there a school on a remote Scottish outpost that only had about five children? The best they could expect would be a tableaux. Something nice and static, no arguing, no shoving and no bloody jazz hands.

I bid Marguerite as cheerful a farewell as I could manage, and set off towards the light of my home, which was now visible in the increasing dark, glowing out of the front windows across the lane, like a beacon calling me in.

7

I sat and stared at my leg.

I didn't think about it as often now as I used to. The whole thing had become second nature to me, and perhaps I kidded myself that it was less noticeable than it had been, now I'd had practice. I didn't limp quite so visibly, I could run a bit, within limits. I had to be careful on slippery surfaces, and walking in snow and ice was difficult, when I couldn't sense whether my foot was going down on something that had no grip, but . . .

But I was still defensive. Still on my guard against those remarks that made me feel like an object. 'Oh, that poor girl, so pretty but having to wear that false leg . . . she'll never be able to go to the beach and wear a bikini . . . the boys won't want to date her, with that great plastic thing strapped on . . . poor girl.' *Poor girl.*

The woodburner crackled and made me jump. It would be nice to say it jolted me out of my self-pity, but it would take more than that to stop the replay going on in my head, a recitation of failed relationships and cut-short dates. I'd come to the conclusion a while back that I wasn't really made for anything long-term, and that the men I really liked were best off without a woman for whom long walks on the beach weren't a romantic proposition, but instead were a series of stumbling obstacles, tiredness and sand-drag.

Was Jake right? Was I being deliberately unpleasant to keep people away? I'd always aimed at 'remote, but polite'. Had I bypassed that and gone straight to 'stand-offish and rude'? Had my attempts to keep myself from being hurt veered into, as he put it, 'being a dick'? Were all those broken relationships and failed dates not because men didn't want a girlfriend who wore a prosthetic, but because they didn't want *me*?

I slumped on the small sofa and rested my head in my hands. Why had nobody told me? Here I was, trying to be all noble and understanding about men not wanting to be landed with a woman who needed help sometimes, but really just pushing away anyone who might care? Paying the price in loneliness? And now, coming to realise, that I was Lydia-the-unsociable rather than Lydia-with-one-leg. Lonely, because I was pretending to protect other people, whilst really protecting myself.

The accident hadn't been spectacular. No tortured, twisted metal and being cut out of a car by the fire brigade, or an illness that had turned to blood poisoning and meant I lost my leg to save my life. Just a rather stupid, drunken encounter with a metal staircase on a wet night in unsuitable shoes. Painful, yes, but no tales to tell of flashing blue lights rushing to the rescue and handsome fire fighters in awe of my self-possession, telling me I'd still be beautiful even after the amputation. None of that. Just exasperated doctors who couldn't work out why my bones wouldn't heal properly, tired nurses moving me from ward to ward, and occasional visits from university friends, who'd gradually all moved on, graduated and left the area, while I struggled with appointments and deferred my placements.

And now I taught in a tiny school, because young children didn't ask questions. Or rather, they did, but only once. And as soon as they heard I'd fallen down some stairs and had to have my leg removed, they lost interest, I became 'Miss', and never had to deal with it again. I kept my head down, worked hard and was just another teacher.

And there was Jake. My body told me I fancied him, my brain admired the way he taught the children and had such a fantastic relationship with them. But my rational mind knew he saw me as a colleague, a member of staff. How else *could* he see me? It's all I was. So I protected myself from the inevitable disappointment by . . . evidently, by being a dick.

My whole face flared with heat and those long-denied tears finally made a proper appearance. I cupped my forehead in my hands and let myself cry until my shoulders were twitching and my breath fell out in great gasps that I had no control over. He was right. He really was right. I could have been fun, sociable and amusing with no intention of any kind of reaction from Jake. I did it with Irina, why couldn't I treat him like I treated other people? Why did I feel I had to punish not only myself, but him too? It wasn't Jake's fault I only had one leg, even if his presence did make me feel more conscious of it.

I was such an idiot.

There was an echoey rap at the door. I'd been so absorbed in my misery that I hadn't noticed any kind of figure approaching and I'd turned off the lamp in the front window, so there hadn't been any shadowy shapes for me to see. I quickly wiped my face on my sleeve and limped to the door, using the furniture for assistance. Maybe Jake had come to . . . not apologise, no. I'd come to realise he had nothing to apologise *for*. But maybe, being the person he was, he'd come to make sure I was all right, even though he probably suspected I'd try to bite him through the letterbox, and maybe throw things at him for even attempting to be nice to me.

Gareth Graham stood on the doorstep, wide smile and innocent blue eyes twinkling in the light that got past me. Snow had started to fall, outlining him against the darkness, and was settling on his hair like a flaky halo. 'Hello, Lydia.'

You're a liar, I thought, but couldn't bring myself to say. 'I'm in the middle of some marking,' I said, figuring that two wrongs might at least set the record straight.

'Oh, I just thought I'd call by. Can I come in?' And before I had chance to use the weight of the metal door to keep him out, he was in my face, then past me, knocking me off balance so I had to grasp at the door handle so as not to fall. I had to swing myself up so that I could grab the back of the nearest chair to help myself move through after him, and found he was already standing in front of the woodburner, rubbing his hands together as though he'd just got home after a long, cold walk. 'Lovely home you have here. Very cosy.'

Those eyes didn't look so friendly now. The smile was less open, more like a guard against words, words I didn't want to hear. 'You can't stay, I have friends coming over in a minute,' I tried. All my skin was standing to attention, poised for me to act, but I couldn't think of a single thing to do, and without my leg on I couldn't move fast enough to get out of the house. On snow I'd get precisely nowhere.

'Oh, that's probably not true, is it?' He sat down on my carefully throw-covered sofa and crossed his legs. 'Do you have any wine? Sherry? I mean, it's the season of goodwill and all that, we should sit and have a drink together.'

He actually patted the seat next to him, like I was an over-anxious dog waiting to be invited onto the couch. 'Come on, calm down, I'm not going to hurt you.'

Really? Because I'm fairly sure you didn't just burst your way in here to sing me two choruses of Silent Night and rattle your collecting tin. I stayed standing, with my knuckles going grey against the cushioning of the chair back. 'I don't have anything in.'

'A week before Christmas and you haven't got any alcohol in the house? What are you waiting for?' Gareth unbuttoned his coat and let it flap loose.

'Tesco,' I replied, shortly. I was running through the floorplan of my little place, trying to think if there was somewhere I could shut myself in, barricade the door and ring for help. But the whole 'open plan' thing, whilst great for decorating, getting around without my prosthetic, and making the place look larger, was a bit light on panic rooms. Even the bathroom didn't have a lock on the door. Why would it need one?

'Well then, why don't you pop the kettle on and we can sit and have a proper chat.' It wasn't a question, but fell just short of being an order. My heart was beating so hard it was a wonder it hadn't impaled itself on my ribcage. 'We should get to know each other a bit better.'

Why had I taken my leg off? At least I could have made an attempt to get away, but as it was I was stuck hopping round the furniture. And I'd left it in the bedroom, so I couldn't even pretend to make tea and put my leg on under the noise of the kettle boiling. 'I want you to go.'

'Aw, come on now.' Gareth lounged comfortably, arms stretched along the sofa back. 'We get on so well, I'm just wanting the chance to get to know all about you.'

All of the no's. The whole of the inside of my head was basically one claxon. *What do I do?* My phone was in the kitchen, on the worktop, I'd have to pretend to make tea and call the police. I started forward, pulling myself along the chair back towards the next support, and suddenly there he was, standing in front of me. He smelled strange, a little musty, as though he'd put his clothes on damp.

'I know you don't really have a grandmother in the White Rose,' I blurted out. 'You're the handyman.'

He sighed. 'Yeah, well. Tell a girl you work part-time fixing some dodgy old geezers' stairlift — well, it's not exactly Richard Branson territory, is it?'

'So you lied?'

A shrug. 'What can I say? Stopped by the school to get directions and fell in love at first sight. Been watching you ever since.'

'That is not love, that is stalking. You don't even know me!'

'Aw, come on! Let's have a cuddle. Or we could just, you know.' He reached out a hand and stroked my hair. 'Fool around.'

I reared back so far that I nearly fell over, and had to clutch towards the table to hold myself up. 'No!'

A moment of silence. The glass on the woodburner ticked, and outside an owl hooted. There was the gentle kind of quiet you get when snow is falling outside, as though even the soundlessness is on mute, almost a white noise. Then he reached out to touch me, I saw his face coming closer, the hand aiming to grab my shoulder, and I knew he was going to try to kiss me. Everything fell into the slow motion reserved for accidents, he was lunging and I was moving back, coming up hard against the table, grabbing behind me at whatever came to hand.

My fingers closed around the box I'd brought back from the Christmas fair. I'd forgotten it, left it on the table awaiting my half-hearted attempt at decorating prior to my solitary Christmas lunch, and as my fingers grasped at it, it tipped. A particularly over-decorated village scene, doubling its weight in glitter and, as Irina had said, 'more robins than a Batman convention', fell into my palm and I didn't even think. I gripped it and swung, and it connected with Gareth's temple in a disco-explosion of sparkles and plastic birds, plaster of Paris splinters flying like fake snow.

There was a *crack*. I didn't know if it had been his head or the plaster, and he dropped to the floor. I hardly dared to look, in case I'd killed him, but a quick check told me that he was out cold on the rug. Breathing, and only a tiny amount of blood, where it looked as though some of the artistically roughened snow had grazed him, which was good enough for me. I hauled myself to the kitchen, grabbed my phone and dialled 999.

I was actually giving my address to the police when there was another knock at the door, and I had to hop over the still fallen Gareth to open it. I didn't even care who was there, I just flung the door wide and hopped back to continue giving my details. Didn't care that someone was going to see me without my leg, didn't care that it could have been *anyone* on the step. With Gareth crumpled on my colour-coordinated rug covered in flakes of plaster and scattered with fallen robins, I somehow felt all-powerful. Probably poisoned with adrenaline, but still, powerful and a little bit super.

'I came to say sor . . . what the hell happened?' It was Jake, peering past me, as I recounted events to the police despatcher on the other end.

'I hit him. He tried to grab me,' I explained.

'Wow.' For a second Jake looked just like Rory Scott, on finding out that I knew all the words to the latest Nicki Minaj song. 'That's . . . impressive. Would you like me to — I don't know, sit on him or something?'

'If you wouldn't mind.' I hung up. The police were on their way. There was a chalkiness in my mouth that told me the adrenaline was leaving, and I probably only had another few moments before I descended into shock, but for now . . . well, for now I was going to use it. 'And you have nothing to apologise for, Jake. You were completely right, I was being a dick. I thought I was just keeping you at a distance, but I didn't have to be quite so . . . '

'Emphatic?' He sat on the rug, firmly on top of Gareth's legs. Gareth was groaning a bit now, but neither of us paid any attention. 'And I didn't have to be quite so offensive. I just . . . look, I really like you, Lydia.'

I realised that I was standing, my legless state obvious, in front of a man I really liked, for the first time ever. I'd never dared take my prosthetic off on a date. Scared that, once they saw my obvious disability, that would be all they'd ever notice about me again, that I would become someone else in their eyes, someone different, other. And here Jake was, and I didn't care. 'I like you too. That's why I was horrible, I didn't want you to think I liked you and have to be all polite about it.'

'Wow,' he said again. 'That's what happens? People you like turn you down?'

'I don't know if they'd turn me down. We never get that far. I just sort of pre-empt any turning down by never putting myself in that position.'

'You're an idiot.' But he said it almost fondly. There was no hint of any kind of pity or suspicion in his eyes, and he was sitting there at knee-level, practically staring into the space where my leg should be.

'Yes, I am. A complete wally. It would just have been horrible to really like you and for you to know it, so it would be all unrequited and having you trying to avoid me and everything.'

Jake glanced down at Gareth, who was starting to make coming round noises. 'Yes. You are clearly very lovable, and anyone who says differently is just asking to be taken out with a plaster of Paris table centrepiece.'

'He tried to kiss me. I didn't even

want him to come in, he just barged past me.'

'I thought you liked me.' Gareth spoke, his voice a little muffled from being face down on the rug. 'I thought we had a connection.'

'Nope. And whatever you thought, it didn't give you the right to come waltzing in here and trying to kiss me. *And* you lied to me about why you were in Heavington, so *not* a level playing field, Gareth.'

'You hit me.'

'Yep. *And* I called the police, so any minute now you can explain to them what you thought you were doing. I don't want to hear it.'

There was a momentary pause, then Gareth said, sulkily, and still into the rug, 'this always happens.'

'You've done this before?' My tone was as icy as the wind currently flipping at the letterbox.

'I'm too nice, that's my trouble, too easy to say 'no' to. But you had tea with me, chatted, reckoned I'd be in with a shout. Thought you might be up for a Friends With Benefits thing, you know. Something casual, just to take you out of yourself, sort of thing.'

'I was being . . . ' I had been going to say 'friendly', but I hadn't even been that, had I? Just used him to try to make Jake jealous. 'Bursting into a woman's house and trying to force her to kiss you isn't the way to go about getting someone to date you, you know?'

'I'm a great kisser.'

'Had a lot of feedback, have we?' Teacher-sarcasm now.

'I practice. On my hand.'

'Can you sit on his head now?' I suggested to Jake, who was staring at Gareth, aghast.

'I reckon you should just hit him again. What sort of an attitude is that?'

I sighed. 'I admit he's on the warped end of the male spectrum, but it happens. Especially if they think you can't get away very quickly.'

Jake shook his head. 'Again, I'm

sorry. On behalf of my entire sex, I apologise. No one should ever have to put up with this kind of thing.' He must have bounced, because Gareth squeaked. 'And I'm sorry if I contributed.'

'No. You were just friendly. I was the one with the attitude.' I sat down on the dining chair and realised, again, that I didn't have my prosthetic on. It surprised me, because I was used to feeling disadvantaged without it, but right now I was still reliving hitting Gareth and my lack of a leg really wasn't featuring. 'I've been playing professional martyr, I think.'

'So you'd actually consider going out with me?' Jake sounded astonished. 'In, like, a relationship format?'

I grinned. 'I'll think about it.'

A blue light strobed along the snow-covered hedge. The local police force didn't have all that much excitement and, this close to Christmas, they were probably spending most of their time fishing drunks out of ditches and stopping fights. A woman with an intruder in her home rated flashing lights and sirens, and I bet they were hating the fact that the snow would have prevented them skidding to a halt with screaming tyres outside my door.

'Let's just hold those thoughts, shall we?' I said. 'I think I might have some explaining to do right now . . . '

8

I woke up early on the morning of the last day of term. A grey, cold kind of light was filtering in through the arched window of my bedroom, and the silence outside was only broken by a robin sitting on the ledge, staring in with an accusatory look on its beak and tweeting pathetically. It was perched on a crust of snow that had thickened in the night to reach nearly halfway up the window, and made most of the table centrepieces look understated.

'Good grief.' I sat up and struggled into my leg, before pulling a dressing-gown on and going into the living room for a proper look. 'There's *feet* of it out there.'

'Feet of what?' Jake sat up under his duvet. He'd been sleeping on the sofa for the last few nights. 'In case Gareth comes back,' he'd said, but I suspected the police warning and a night in the cells had put paid to any intentions Gareth might have had. Plus being hit around the head with a plaster model village would have left him in no doubt that my affections, as they say, lay elsewhere.

'Snow. It's snowed again in the night. A lot.' I tried to ignore the fact that Jake had no shirt on, and was revealing a large acreage of quite hairy chest as he wriggled around to look out of the window.

'Ah.' Then he grinned. 'Am I going to have to carry you to school?'

I gave him a stern look. 'I'm fine, if I can just lean on your arm. No carrying.'

'Are you sure?' And, dropping the duvet, he bent and picked me up. 'I quite fancy carrying you in.'

This was the closest he'd come to me, apart from holding my hand on the sofa while we'd watched TV, and a peck on the cheek as a goodnight kiss. For a second I almost panicked. The power-lessness of being off my feet, that sensation of loss of control over my own body flowed over my head and made me grab onto his arm. But then other sensations cut in, the feel of his chest against my cheek and shoulder. The muscles of his bare arm under my hand. The spark in his eyes as he grinned at me again and lifted me higher and whispered 'I hid all the table decorations last night,' and lowered his mouth down onto mine. And, before I knew it, the feel of his hair in my hands, the cool slide of his skin against mine and the lack of breath as I whispered his name.

'We're going to be late for school.'

'In this, so is everyone else.' He laid me down on my bed and, before I knew it, we were tangled in one another, making the kind of energetic love that comes from two people who have spent too much time correcting spellings, policing a Wendy house and getting their pockets ripped by vindictive door handles. It was unexpected, but lovely. Jake was gentle, but not too gentle, he didn't make me feel as though he thought I might break if he made any sudden moves, and the whole experience was thoroughly satisfactory.

'The children are going to know something's happened,' I said, when we finally made it out of bed and the bread was in the toaster. 'Expect lots of daft rhymes, and Rory chanting Beyoncé lyrics at you.'

'I'm going to have to take him to one side and tell him it's not 'all the simple ladies', aren't I?' Jake pushed his hair back. 'It's like being dad to eleven kids. And they don't have to know about *this*. We can tell them we're a couple, though, can't we?'

'Are we?'

'Aren't we? They've noticed us pitching up at school together these past few days and I've told Mrs Dobson to put the cheese and potato pie on hold for a bit.'

'Let's just get to school, shall we? We

might have to do some recasting before the evening's performance, if the snow's bad enough that some people can't get in, and those sugar plums won't sort themselves out.'

It was worse than I'd thought outside. The snow was about three feet deep, it must have snowed all evening and all night, but Jake and I had been watching TV, drinking wine and laughing, so we hadn't even noticed it start. The sky was heavy and the kind of yellowish-grey that spoke of more snow to come, and we plodded our careful way along the lane towards school. Not a single vehicle attempted the road, not even some of the bigger 4×4's were out. The only tracks were from a tractor, heading out to feed stock and, when we reached school, only Alan was in.

'Irina can't get in, and the main road is closed,' he said. 'We're going to have to close the school and cancel tonight.'

Jake's face fell so far that you'd have thought Alan had said he was going to cancel Christmas. 'But we can't!' he said. 'The village kids will still be here.'

'And the White Rose folks are so looking forward to it,' I added, remembering Marguerite and her eagerness. She'd already been in to talk to Alan about some kind of reciprocal visiting arrangements, and he'd leaped on her offer for residents to come in and listen to children read. 'More than Christmas, I think.'

Alan pondered for a moment. 'Well, we were opening later today to account for everyone being up late for the performance this evening, so let's give it a while and see who can get in. I'll phone the farm and ask Mr Dobson to scrape the lane clear as far as White Rose, and we'll just hope for no more snow beforehand. It would be a shame to have to cancel when everyone's worked so hard.' He flapped his tie in an Oliver Hardy sort of way. 'You two look very perky today. Excited about Christmas?'

I looked at the huge tree in the hall, decorated with baubles and wound with unnecessarily glamorous lights and tinsel. Amid the stacked chairs, discarded coats, left-behind reading bags and the packed-lunch trolley, it looked like a stripper in a cow barn. And I thought about this morning, with Jake. About his arms around me and his kiss on my lips. 'Yes, I suppose we are,' I said.

'We're spending Christmas together,' Jake said. 'What with the two of us being the only two single people here.'

'Are we?'

'Aren't we?'

We looked at each other. Alan continued to fiddle with his tie. 'I suppose we are,' I said again. 'After all, we've got a house full of table centrepieces to use up.' The thought of waking up on Christmas morning was suddenly appealing. Rather than Christmas feeling like an ordeal that had to be undergone, a day that had to pass, it was suddenly full of shadowy promise, like a bulky Christmas stocking waiting to be unpacked. 'Yes, we are,' I said again, more firmly.

Jake grinned. 'Of course we are.'

'Right. Right.' Alan didn't seem to know where to look, so he examined his tie again. 'Well. Let's get things sorted for tonight then, although I have to say, I rather think cancelling might be a better idea, but I'm not going to close the school whilst some of us are here.'

We headed off to our respective classrooms, to await any overexcited children who might manage to struggle in through the snow, but when it became evident, with the arrival of Rory, telling us that the main roads were completely blocked, that we weren't going to get many, we amalgamated in my classroom. Which was just as well, because we ended up with just the village eight: Rory Scott, Sarah and James Cowton and the five Grace children.

Jake, Alan and I looked over our tiny flock. 'Well,' Jake said, philosophically, 'I think the moon tap-dance is out.'

Alan shook his head. 'We have to cancel. It's ridiculous.'

I surprised myself then. 'No, we

can't. The White Rose people will come anyway, it's an outing for them, and as long as they get to see some cute children doing things in costume, they'll be happy. Tea and mince pies afterwards, like we planned, Rory's brought in about a tonne of Christmas muffins — we can do it. We can make this an event to remember.'

'It's going to be forgetting it afterwards that's the challenge,' Jake said.

The two men looked at me. I looked at the children. Rory, Timothy and Oscar were cleaning my whiteboard, Sarah and James were playing with some building blocks, and Aurora, Atticus and Celeste Grace had found the dressing up clothes and were dancing around the room draped in various garments. 'We can do it,' I said again, firmly.

'Are you sure?' Alan said, in a wobbly sort of way. 'I mean, eight children . . . is it enough?'

'And three adults,' I said. 'Okay, we'll have to scale back on 'children going to bed' and, Jake, you're going to have to double up, but we've got our lead character, and our Father Christmas, if I do the narration and play a couple of parts, and we run everyone through some quick clothing changes, I think we'll be all right.'

Jake drew me to one side. 'Are you sure?' he asked, in a completely different way to Alan. 'Narrating and everything? I thought you didn't want to be centre of anyone's attention?'

I have a feeling that the look I gave him was slightly pitying. 'This is putting on *The Night Before Christmas* to an audience so small that we could probably hold the performance in Alan's office. Not Saturday Night at the London Palladium.'

'Yes, but . . . '

'I have to start somewhere. Start *again* somewhere, I mean. Perhaps this is nature's way of telling me to sort myself out. Stop feeling sorry for myself and trying to blend into the background all the time.'

'I think that makes nature sound a little bit vindictive actually.' Jake gave me a grin. 'Here you are, reinventing yourself!'

'In front of about nine people.'

'Baby steps, baby steps.'

I clapped my hands and got the children's attention. 'Right chaps. The play is going to go on, but we're going to need you lot to listen very carefully . . . '

'All *right*!' said Rory, enthusiastically, and punched the air.

'I can shake my belly,' said Oscar, with relish. 'I've been practising.'

'That's good.'

Celeste's little lip was wobbling. 'Am I still going to do my dance?' she asked. 'I want mummy to see me doing my dance.' She clung on to Sarah Cowton, whose lower lip was dangerously close to the floor too. 'We want to do our dance!'

'You are going to dance. You are also going to get to be reindeer and put stockings up on the fireplace. Let's get

146

the bag of costumes, and we'll sort this thing out.'

Jake, from where he was sitting perched on my desk, whispered to me as I went off to find the costume bag, where it had been hung up in the staff room. 'You are so masterful. I think I like it.'

'And Mister Immingham is going to be a reindeer too! Won't that be fun?' I called over my shoulder as I left the room. I had to imagine his expression, but the thought made me smile, as I sorted out the bag with the floppy antlers and the oversized beard, and went back for an emergency costume fitting and cast reappraisal.

9

The hall, small as it was, wasn't exactly full. The front row contained Mr and Mrs Cowton, the Grace parents, plus Bo-Bo, and the Scotts. Behind them, and tripling our audience, were the nine White Rose residents plus five of the house staff. Everyone was wearing their best clothes, albeit under layers of coat and wellington boots. There were even some fancy hats. Marguerite, I saw, was wearing a feather fascinator, as if she was off to a wedding, and there was a degree of raucous chat breaking out, a lot of it involving Bo-Bo burbling and being cooed over by a trio of old ladies. Mince pie crumbs were everywhere, and I made a mental note to drop a box of chocolates in to Mrs Wilkinson after the performance was over. Mr Scott had his phone out, and was obviously set to record his son's stage debut, I thought about asking him to put it away but decided not to bother. Rory was going to act his young socks off, and it deserved to be filed away for posterity.

I stood backstage. 'No, no, you look lovely,' I said to Jake, who, in his initial capacity as The Wife was wearing a nightshirt hastily contrived from an old sheet, and a nightcap which was actually Father Christmas's red Santa hat turned inside out. We'd worked out some lightning costume changes, which were going to make some elements of the play come over more in the line of a French farce, but The Show Would Go On.

'And you make a great mouse.'

I'd squeezed myself into the grey onesie that Jonah North was to have worn. The legs finished halfway up my calves, and made my prosthetic very evident but we had more to worry about right now than a plastic leg. The sugar plums, all four of them, were having collective stage fright in the girls' toilet. 'I try.'

'Very cute.' He touched the tip of my nose.

'Thank you. Now, get on stage and settle your brain for a long winter nap.'

'Think I'd rather be a sugar plum,' he muttered. But his eyes were shining as he said it, and I knew he didn't care how ridiculous he looked, as long as the children got to perform.

'It might come to that, if we can't get them out of the loo.' I blew him a kiss and regretted it when Rory, bouncing up and down in his rather better fitting nightshirt, squealed.

'Miss just kissed Mister Immingham!'

'It's going to come out sooner or later,' Jake said to me, and then adjusted the sheet, 'And there's definitely going to be an element of something coming out sooner rather than later, in this costume.'

'Onstage. Now.'

And *The Night Before Christmas* happened, as magically as was possible.

I narrated and moused, curled up in the middle of the stage. Alan was a rather oversized child asleep in his bed, the stockings were hung with theatrical care by the cast, those not already night-shirted were draped in sheets and sleeping bags as nightwear. The sugar plums' dancing was backed by some rather falsetto singing by Jake and Alan, while Aurora Grace helped out her younger brother and sister and Sarah and James, by being a rather tall sugar plum in a rather undersized costume, so much of her dance was performed in a half-crouched position. There was a brief moment of panic when James caught sight of his mother in the audience and froze, but he soon went back to twirling and singing again. We were a little under-reindeered, and those we had were a rather patchwork assortment of colours, being played by Alan and Jake wearing nightshirts and antlers, Timothy in a proper reindeer costume, and Aurora, Atticus and Sarah all still wearing their sugar plum gear and antlers. Oscar wore the full Father Christmas regalia and managed a good 'Happy Christmas to all, and to all a

Good Night', whilst showing off his prowess at wobbling his belly again, and the round of applause that resulted belied our tiny audience by being resounding and heartfelt.

Afterwards, we all ate mince pies, drank tea and enjoyed the adulation. The White Rose crew had a whale of a time congratulating the children, cuddling Bo-Bo (whose name, apparently, was Lysander) and generally behaving like a massed ensemble of grandparents. Marguerite took me to one side as I clambered off the stage and told me that they hoped we'd do a play every year from now on, as they'd found it such a refreshing change from spending the night before Christmas Eve watching Hercule Poirot films and eating mint thins. I had to agree that we'd do something similar next year, only hopefully without the restricted cast and lightning costume changes that we'd had inflicted on us this year.

And then it was all over, and we turned out the lights, leaving the school to its cabbage smells, its paper chains and its silence, and Jake and I walked back up the snow-filled lane to my little house.

The woodburner was still glowing, the lamps threw long, golden flares onto the snow and the place smelled of warmth and still-drying plaster of Paris. Jake had decorated a bare branch with an assortment of hanging baubles as made by the children, and propped it in one corner, where it had shed glitter until it looked like a gaunt glam-rock star up to his knees in a pool.

We stood together in the little living room and looked at one another. Jake was still wearing his antlers and I'd got Timothy's Father Christmas hat on.

'In the immortal words of Roy Wood, I wish it could be Christmas every day,' Jake turned and put his arms around me. 'This is amazing. Tonight was amazing. I'd like to stay like this forever — you, the firelight, the snow and all that. I am so glad that you managed to . . .'

'Stop being a dick?' I returned his hug.

'I was going to say, that you managed to come to terms with things a little bit, but yes, now you mention it, I'm glad of that too.' He gave me a kiss, which started as a passing peck on the lips, but extended until we were wrapped around each other.

Eventually we broke apart. 'Of course, there is one problem,' I said.

'I'm not seeing it.' He moved a bit closer. 'This is practically perfect from where I'm standing. So, what is it?'

I raised an eyebrow. 'Which one of our millions of table centrepieces are we going to use for Christmas dinner?' With a wave I indicated the white plaster mountain, glitter prisming in the lamplight and the assorted plastic robins all regarding us with identical beady eyes. Tiny white plaster houses decorated with cotton wool snow sat lumpily on bark-shedding bits of tree trunk. We had a lifetime's worth of ornamentation.

'No contest.' He picked up the one on the top. Its plaster was shredded, revealing the framework inside, the glitter had all gone and only one robin remained, at a drunken angle, clinging to one side of the plaster cone. It was the decoration I'd used to hit Gareth over the head. 'This one. It's symbolic.'

'It's lopsided, is what it is.'

Jake lifted me off my feet, sweeping the Father Christmas hat from my head and placing it down on top of the chosen decoration. 'So are you, Lydia, my love,' he said. 'But you are gorgeous, nonetheless!' And he carried me through to the bedroom, to start the Christmas holidays in style.

Thank you

Thank you for reading! I hope you enjoyed spending time with Lydia and Jake, and the rest of Heavington village, and you now feel suitably Christmassy and ready to engage with crackers and pudding. Hopefully, your table centrepieces won't be nearly as combative as the one in the story.

Can I take this opportunity to wish you a peaceful, happy and fun-filled Christmas.

We do hope that you have enjoyed reading this large print book.

Did you know that all of our titles are available for purchase?

We publish a wide range of high quality large print books including:
**Romances, Mysteries, Classics
General Fiction
Non Fiction and Westerns**

Special interest titles available in large print are:
**The Little Oxford Dictionary
Music Book, Song Book
Hymn Book, Service Book**

Also available from us courtesy of Oxford University Press:
**Young Readers' Dictionary
(large print edition)
Young Readers' Thesaurus
(large print edition)**

For further information or a free brochure, please contact us at:
**Ulverscroft Large Print Books Ltd.,
The Green, Bradgate Road, Anstey,
Leicester, LE7 7FU, England.
Tel:** (00 44) **0116 236 4325
Fax:** (00 44) **0116 234 0205**

EMERGENCY NURSE

Phyllis Mallet

Nurse Marion Talbot and Doctor Alan
Vincent work together in Casualty.
Marion is drawn to him a little more
every day — but wonders what she
can do to attract his attention. Then
they each reveal they will have a relative visiting soon: Marion her mother,
and Alan his uncle; and so they hatch
a plan to give them a good time,
while deciding to meet up themselves.
But when a nurse from the hospital
is attacked, and the police become
involved, things do not run as smoothly
as they had anticipated . . .